HANGMAN'S LEGACY

Also by Frederic Bean

Tom Spoon

HANGMAN'S LEGACY

Frederic Bean

Walker and Company
New York

To my father,
Kenneth L. Bean

First published in the United States of America in 1991
by Walker Publishing Company, Inc.

Published simultaneously in Canada by Thomas Allen & Son
Canada, Limited, Markham, Ontario

Library of Congress Cataloging-in-Publication Data
Bean, Frederic, 1944–
Hangman's legacy / Frederic Bean.
p. cm.
ISBN 0-8027-4117-7
I. Title.
[PS3552.E152H36 1990]
813'.54—dc20   90-27717
CIP

Printed in the United States of America

2 4 6 8 10 9 7 5 3 1

CHAPTER 1

HOBART Shedd glanced at the faces around him. Even in the poor light the ranch foreman could tell which of his men were morbidly curious and which were just plain scared.

"Cut him down, Mingus," Hob said gently. "Some of the rest of you can look for some soft ground so we can bury him."

Mingus Strawn swung out of his saddle. It was so quiet that Hob could hear the creak of his partner's saddle leather. Mingus handed another cowboy his reins, then walked stiffly to the cottonwood tree, his spurs rattling over the caliche hardpan until he stood beneath the dead man's boots. Mingus opened his pocketknife and cut the rope. There was a heavy thud when the body fell.

"You could'a caught him, Mingus," Shorty Stewart said softly.

"Didn't see no need, seein' as he's dead," Mingus replied.

All eyes were on the sun-stiffened corpse lying below the cottonwood limb. A pale quarter-moon shone on the dead man's face. They had found the body twisting in a soft night breeze just after sundown, at the end of a long day branding calves as they headed back to the chuck wagon.

"Poor bastard," Shorty intoned from his perch atop a bay gelding. "Hell of a way to die."

"Reckon who done it, Hob?" Mingus asked, without taking his eyes from the slipknot around the dead man's neck.

"Hard to say," Hob replied thoughtfully. "Come daylight, we'll take a look at the tracks."

Hob glanced across the river. Beyond the shallow current was Mexico.

1

"I'll lay odds he was a wanted man," Tip Giles said, commanding the attention of every cowboy when he spoke, since everyone knew wanted men was a subject Tip could discuss with authority. He had come to the Barclay ranch four years earlier as a wanted man himself, running from his past as a hired killer. But the years of relative peace as a working cowboy had done little to allay Tip's caution. He was continually looking over his shoulder, and his dark face was deeply etched with lines of concern. "Somebody caught up with him just before he made the river. Looks like they decided to hang him instead of take him back."

An uneasy silence followed while the Bar B riders gave consideration to Tip's remark. Hob noticed that Scoop Singleton seemed a mite paler than usual, even in the dark.

"Mingus, you and Scoop see that he gets buried," Hob said. "Check his pockets to see if there's anything that'll tell us who he was. See you back at the wagon."

Hob reined his dun gelding away from the tree and struck a trot, followed by the others who were not detailed to the burial. As Hob guided his horse through the night shadows, he contemplated the sudden turn of events. In the half dozen years since he came to work for Tom Barclay, he had seen some mighty strange goings-on, but in all those years not one man had been hanged on the Barclay spread. He had come west when the war was over to look for the most peaceful spot on earth, determined to remove himself from places where men killed each other. Over the years there had been a few scrapes with Indians and Mexican bandits, but for the most part, life at the Bar B gave him the peace and quiet he wanted.

Now there was a dead man to account for that would distract the men from ranch chores. Not a word was said among the men who rode behind him as they crossed the moonlit flats. The memory of the corpse at the end of the hangman's rope kept them silent until they neared the ravine where Cookie's campfire flickered beside the chuck wagon.

Hob rode to the fire and swung down. Cookie Bascom peered around the back of the wagon wearing his perpetual sour expression, watching Hob approach the simmering stewpot.

"What the hell kept you?" Cookie asked, slamming a spoon into the chuck box with unnecessary force.

Hob ignored the remark, smelling chilis and stewed meat and a faintly sweet odor he didn't recognize.

"What's for supper?" Hob asked, eyeing the Dutch oven set to one side of the fire.

"Burnt stew," Cookie grumbled, wiping his hands on the front of his apron. "It was good stew an hour ago. Now it's burnt."

"We were delayed," Hob muttered, searching for a tin coffee cup in the dishpan. "Found a dead man. Somebody hanged him."

Cookie halted on his way to the fire, searching Hob's face.

"A dead man?" he asked, as if he hadn't heard Hob right the first time.

"Hung in a tree," Hob replied softly as he poured boiling coffee from the smoke-blackened pot. "Been dead a day or two, judgin' by the stiffness."

"Who is he?" Cookie asked carefully.

"He didn't give us his name."

Cookie uttered a cussword under his breath. "You know what I meant, Hob. Was he anybody from around these parts?"

Hob shook his head, blowing steam from his cup. "Never saw him before. A stranger to this country. I told Mingus to search his pockets, to see if he carried anything that'll tell us who he was."

"Damn," Cookie muttered, frowning. "Who the hell would go to all the trouble of hangin' a feller way out here in the middle of nowhere?"

Hob shrugged, sipping coffee that was hot enough to scald the hide off his tongue. "Hard to say, Cookie. Tip figures he was a wanted man, and when the bunch that was after him caught up, they strung him up. Could be he was an outlaw. Whoever hanged him didn't leave us a note telling why they left him decoratin' that tree."

Cookie made a face. "It ain't funny, Hob. Can't see no humor in it a'tall."

Hob gave Cookie a warning look. "Nobody's laughing, Cookie. It was you who asked all the damn fool questions. Let's eat some of that burnt stew. My belly is rubbin' against my backbone."

Hob set his coffee aside and began to strip his saddle from the dun. One by one, the other men came toward the fire, dragging saddles to the circle of firelight after their horses were picketed in the ravine.

Cookie removed tin plates from the dishpan and set them in rows on a plank near the fire while Hob took his horse to the picket line. When he returned the men were gathered around the fire to ladle stew into their plates, still without their usual banter. It was Hob's guess that the dead man had silenced their tongues. He had to admit it had been a grisly sight when they rode up on the tree at dusk.

The men settled against their saddles to eat. For a time the sounds of scraping spoons rattled eerily around the camp. Not a word was exchanged among them. It was the quietest supper Hob could remember since he came to work for Tom Barclay.

"Cheerful bunch, ain't they?" Cookie asked when Hob tossed his plate in the dishpan.

Hob was spared from having to offer a reply when the sounds of horses echoed from the south. "That'll be Mingus and Scoop," he said, gazing toward the sound.

"There's plum pie in the Dutch oven," Cookie said. "It's a good thing I found a wild plum bush when we crossed that dry creek this mornin', because this outfit appears to be in need of something to sweeten up the mood it's in. You too, Hob."

Hob acknowledged Cookie's remark with a tip of his hat brim, watching Mingus and Scoop ride through the night shadows to the picket line. Any other time, wild plum pie would have been a nice variation from Cookie's regular menu, but finding the dead man had affected his appetite. Hob had hardly tasted the plate of stew.

Mingus's face was ashen when he came to the fire. Scoop was the color of snow. Everyone was watching the pair as they took helpings of stew, awaiting news about the contents of the dead man's pockets.

"Find anything on him?" Hob asked when Mingus was seated beside the fire.

Mingus shoveled food into his cheeks, then nodded and said, "A letter. Found it in one of his boots."

Hob got up and came over to Mingus with his hand outstretched. Mingus reached into a shirt pocket and drew out a wrinkled envelope. Hob took the letter and walked to the fire, opening it with a callused hand, frowning at the scribbled lines.

"Somebody'll have to help Hob," Soap Osborn declared. "He can't read a word. One time, down in El Paso, we walked up to this cantina where we saw a big sign. I asked Hob what the sign said, and he told me it was nothing to worry about . . . that it was only the name of the place. We ended up getting ourselves arrested. That sign said it was against the law to bring a gun inside."

Some of the men laughed. Hob ignored it, squinting at the yellowed page. It was true that he couldn't read much, what with just two years of schooling, but he could make out a sizable number of words if they weren't the fancy two-dollar variety. He'd gotten by for most of his thirty-four years in passable fashion. A cowboy didn't need to decipher more than a hatful of words in the first place.

"It says here on this envelope that this letter is addressed to Dave Cobb, at a place called Prairie Hill," Hob began. "That's what it says. Then it goes like this: 'Dear Dave, we buried the loot over in Mexico. You know the place. Ride to the back of the canyon. When you git to the spring, look east. You can see the cave where we buried Jack. In the cave, at the back, is where we buried your share of the bank loot. Good luck. I bought me a ranch down in Torreon if you care to pay me a call.' Signed Roy."

Hob held the letter for a time, reading it again to himself.

"Dave Cobb," Mingus said softly. "Appears we buried a bank robber."

Hob shook his head silently, wondering.

"Can't figure who hanged him," Mingus added.

"Maybe the law was following him, looking for the money," Tip offered.

"Whoever it was didn't find this letter, or they'd have kept it," Hob said. "It tells how to find the bank loot. In a canyon, it says, near a spring where they buried a feller named Jack."

"Wonder how much it was?" Shorty asked absently, toying with a spur.

"No tellin'," Hob replied, as though the question was addressed to him. "This feller Cobb must have thought it was enough to ride all the way out here with this letter in his boot. Can't quite figure who would have hung him, unless it was somebody who know'd about the money and wanted it for himself. Somebody could have followed from a distance, I reckon, until Cobb got to the river. It still don't figure why they hung Cobb. Maybe he wouldn't tell where he was headed."

Tip shook off the notion quickly. "They would have kept followin' him until he dug up the loot," Tip said. "It don't make sense that they'd have hung Cobb beforehand."

"Would make more sense to wait," Hob agreed.

"Wonder how much money is buried down there?" Shorty asked again. "I say we ride over and have ourselves a look . . . maybe dig it up for ourselves. We could quit this outfit an' live like rich folks down in Mexico for the rest of our days, if we can find that money."

Hob discounted the idea. "Wouldn't be right, Shorty. The money wouldn't be ours. It says in the letter that it's bank loot. We'd have to find out which bank got robbed and give it back to 'em."

"Could be there's a reward," Soap Osborn added quickly. "Over in Pecos I saw this big reward poster offerin' a thousand dollars for some bank loot robbed by John Wesley Hardin. Maybe ol' Cobb rode with Hardin? Could be this is the same money they're talkin' about on that poster."

Hob shrugged, wondering. The Barclay ranch ran for miles along the Rio Grande. Mexico was a haven for all manner of outlaws. It was possible that Cobb was a member of the Hardin Gang who rode back to claim his share of the loot from a big bank robbery. Too, there were others who robbed banks in other parts of the state who rode hell-for-leather toward Mexico where the Texas Rangers couldn't follow.

"There's work to be done on this ranch," Hob said. "Tom Barclay ain't payin' us to wander all over the place looking for buried money. In case you've forgot, we get paid to work cattle on this spread."

"Aw hell, Hob," Shorty protested, "we could all make rich men of ourselves if we find that money. Workin' for wages, we'll die broke. I say we ride over and take a look. Won't take but a day or so."

Hob shook his head, this time with more resolve. "Wouldn't be fair to Tom," he said. "I'd have to answer to the boss for the days we didn't work. Maybe, after we get the calves branded, we could ride over to Ojinaga and rest up for a day or so. Drink some tequila and pay a visit on the girls, I suppose. Tom wouldn't mind, if the calves were all branded. If some of you took a hankerin' to look for the bank loot right then, I wouldn't have no objection."

"Me and Shorty will go," Soap said, grinning across the fire at his partner. The news didn't surprise Hob. Soap and Shorty had been partners since they hired on at the ranch, and were often accused of being in each other's shadow. They had similar dispositions, and both had a fondness for whiskey and fistfights. They were good cowboys when there was work to be done, but they showed an inclination toward wilder pursuits when they had some time off.

"I'd like to ride along too, Hob," Scoop said, looking to Hob for approval. "I sure could use a share of that reward."

"Reckon I'll go along with 'em too," Mingus offered, glancing sheepishly in Hob's direction.

"I ain't gonna be left out, " Cookie shouted from the back of his wagon. "I'm goin' along. We can leave this chuck wagon at Ojinaga 'til we get back."

Hob studied the faces of his men in the firelight. Only Tip had been silent about joining the search for the buried money. As foreman at the Bar B, it was Hob's decision. Almost to a man, the cowboys wanted to look for the buried treasure.

"What makes you so all-fired sure you can find it?" Hob asked. "This letter don't say all that much. There's a thousand canyons over in Mexico. We could look for a month of Sundays and never find the right one."

It was Mingus who offered the first solution.

"We ride due south from here, Hob." he said. "This was where ol' Dave Cobb aimed to cross the Rio Grande. We ride south and look for a canyon with a spring. We look for the grave where the gent called Jack is buried and a cave. We can scatter out so's we can cover some country. I don't figure it'll take no time at all to ride right up on it."

A murmur of agreement went around the campfire, until Tip Giles cleared his throat and continued, "You boys are forgettin' one thing. The gents who hung Mr. Cobb—might be they're down there too, pokin' around for that money. We could get our necks stretched by the same bunch."

Soap stood up quickly, always the first to look for a fight. "We can just shoot the sons of bitches," he said, resting a palm on the butt of his pistol. "There's near 'bout a dozen of us. Cobb was just one man."

Tip shrugged when he heard Soap's remark. It was common knowledge among the Bar B hands that Tip had ridden west from San Antonio ahead of a posse to escape his past as a shootist. Tip carried a modified Colt on his right leg, tied low in a cutaway holster. When it came to guns, Tip's opinion was always regarded higher than any other on the ranch, even though he no longer made his living with his pistol.

"The men who hung Cobb ain't been counted," Tip said. "Could be there's more'n a dozen of them."

His grim pronouncement silenced the men for a time. They exchanged glances, listening to the crackle of the fire.

"Tomorrow we'll be able to tell by the tracks around that cottonwood tree," Soap declared, looking around for support. "Count the tracks that ain't ours. That way we'll know how many we're up against."

When Tip had nothing more to offer, Shorty agreed with Soap. "Good idea. We can count the tracks," he said.

Hob considered the proposition again, wondering what sort of folly they'd be riding into if they looked for the money. The men had a few days coming after so many weeks of gathering wild bunches of longhorns across the ranch. A day or two wandering empty canyons below the river wouldn't do much harm, unless Tip was right about the men who hanged Dave Cobb. One thing was painfully clear: whoever hanged Cobb was serious about finding the buried loot. Dead serious.

Hob folded the letter carefully and stuck it in his shirt pocket. He would hold off making a decision until the tracks were counted tomorrow morning.

"We'll see," he said softly, gazing up at the stars. It was a clear night, so they wouldn't have to worry about a sudden storm washing out the hoofprints. "In the morning, we'll scout the area. If there ain't too many tracks around that tree, we'll head west to Ojinaga after we finish branding and take a few days off. Can't see as it'll hurt anything, I don't reckon."

Hob poured himself another cup of coffee and walked away from the fire to check the horses. He heard spurs jingling and recognized the sound. Mingus was following him.

"Wait up, Hob," he said, speaking softly, as if he had something important to say. "There's somethin' I ain't told you. I can't swear to it, seein' as it was so dark, but whilst me an' Scoop was digging that grave I thought I saw a man sittin' his horse on the far side of the river. It was too dark to be sure, but it could have been a man on a horse. I didn't say anything to the kid, mainly because he was already spooked by bein' around a dead man."

Hob gazed south, toward the silent black hills of Mexico. Mingus had always been disposed to flights of fancy. He was, without a doubt, the most superstitious cowboy with the outfit. When the moon was full, Mingus dutifully poured salt in his left boot to keep ghosts from disturbing his slumber, a remedy provided by his grandmother before Mingus left Fort Smith to seek his fortunes in Texas.

There were other harbingers of certain doom Mingus feared: a horseshoe turned the wrong way; dappled gray horses with blue eyes; walking under ladders, and so forth. Hob had grown accustomed to his partner's many rituals observed to avoid unleashing all manner of bad luck, and he doubted Mingus had seen anyone on the Mexican side of the river. They were fifty miles or more from the closest ranch or town on either side of the Rio Grande. Months would pass without another living soul showing up, especially in winter. Fall was drawing near, and it was unlikely that anyone would be riding the vast empty wastes of the Rio Grande border country.

Then Hob remembered the body they had found swaying in a gentle breeze, dangling at the end of a lariat. There had been at least two visitors to Bar B range. Dave Cobb—and whoever hanged him.

CHAPTER 2

"I'VE got it figured this way," Hob said, squatting on his haunches beneath the cottonwood limb where yesterday Dave Cobb dangled from a rope. "The gent who was following Cobb got too close when they reached the river. Cobb spotted him and got set to put up a fight. There are empty shell casings behind the tree trunk to prove there was a gunfight. When Cobb's gun was empty, the feller rushed him. There are signs of a scuffle in the dirt right over there."

The Bar B hands studied the ground, following Hob's finger as he pointed to the tracks and the empty shells. No one could offer a better explanation for the hanging.

"Ain't but one set of tracks," Mingus said softly, swinging a look around the riverbank. "Just one man. It don't figure why he went to all the trouble of hangin' Cobb. A bullet would have been easier."

"I'd guess it was the work of a man lookin' for revenge," Tip said. "Hangin's one hell of a way to die."

Coming from Tip, the judgment had considerable weight, because dying was a subject he knew a thing or two about, according to the stories that followed him from San Antonio.

Hob stood up and walked to the water's edge where the tracks of two horses entered the shallows. "He took Cobb's horse and crossed into Mexico. This feller, whoever he is, he knows the money is buried somewhere on the Mexican side of the river. He's liable to be over there now, making his try at finding the loot."

The cowboys spent a quiet moment looking across the Rio Grande. Hob considered the possibility that the man Mingus said he had seen was the one who killed Dave Cobb. He

11

didn't like the idea that the killer might have been watching them yesterday from across the river. Instinctively, he checked his gunbelt. His Colt .44/.40 sat against his leg, snug in its worn holster. Hob couldn't remember when he last needed the six-gun, but he was glad it was there now.

"Let's ride over and have a look-see," Shorty said, squinting into the morning sunlight. "We can see which direction the owlhoot rode when he reached the other side."

Hob frowned, briefly studying his reflection on the smooth surface of the river. His faded bib-front shirt was now a pale blue, the same color as his eyes. The shirt had been mended in countless places, as had his worn denims, thanks to the skillful hands of Tom Barclay's wife, Clara. His hat was sweat-stained around the crown, shading his leathery face from the sun, casting a shadow over a week's worth of black whiskers. He knew he needed a bath—he wondered if the day of the week might be Saturday. He'd lost all track of time during the branding. The days seemed to run together.

"We've got more calves to brand," he said, although his tone was halfhearted when he spoke. He, too, wanted to see the tracks on the Mexican side of the river. "I reckon we could ride over, just to see what's there."

"Now you're talking, Hob," Shorty exclaimed, spurring his bay toward the river. "We can catch up on branding those calves when we get back."

"Hold on," Hob admonished, swinging a leg over his dun. "We ain't gonna go off half-cocked on some treasure hunt. Let's just have a look at those tracks before we decide."

Mingus grunted, urging his roan alongside Hob.

"We're near 'bout done with the branding, Hob. Couldn't be more'n a few left without a brand."

Hob felt a gnawing uneasiness as he rode into the shallows. The search for buried bank loot would anger Tom Barclay if he knew about it, but the men had earned a few days of pleasure after so many weeks in the saddle. The branding was rough work, and even before yesterday Hob had promised them a few nights in Ojinaga when the work was done. So what if they took a short break before they finished? And what difference did it make how the men spent the time they had coming to them? If they chose to waste it looking for buried money in Mexico, the choice was theirs to make, he supposed.

It was late fall and the Rio Grande was seasonally low, so the crossing was easy enough. When they rode out on the sandy bank, the horses shook themselves to rid water from their coats. Hob kept his eye on the pair of hoofprints leading away from the river, following them across a stretch of foothills until they went out of sight in the brush.

"Due south, like I figured," Mingus said, eyeing the tracks.

Hob stood in his stirrups for a better view of the hills. He could see rocky mesas off in the distance. The rocks would hide a thousand canyons. It would be like looking for a needle in a haystack, finding the right one. Hob reined his dun to a halt, squinting at the horizon.

"A man could get lost down there," he said, "if he don't know the lay of things. Liable to stir up an Indian or two . . . maybe Mexican bandits, if he ain't careful. We've lost a few cattle over the years. A man oughta stay careful."

Mingus frowned, making a study of the landscape. "Looks mighty empty, Hob."

Hob swung a look at his men. Cookie sat on a borrowed sorrel. He wore a gunbelt around his waist, as if he aimed to go along with the others.

"Who's going, and who's stayin'?" Hob asked.

Hands went quickly into the air. All but Tip indicated a preference for the ride.

"Suits me," Hob said. "Me an' Tip will go back and get the saddle string and the chuck wagon. Then we'll head for Ojinaga. I'm allowin' two days for this wild-goose chase. Two days, mind you, and then you have yourselves over to Ojinaga ready to come back to finish the branding. Understood?"

Heads nodded agreement. Cookie jerked a thumb over his

shoulder, pointing to a pair of burlap bags tied behind his saddle. "Didn't bring but enough chuck fer two days, Hob," he said. "These jaspers will be ready to pull out soon as the food runs out. See you in Ojinaga."

Mingus rode over to Hob and held out his hand. "I figure we should take that letter, Hob, so's we can find the landmarks when we get to the right canyon."

Hob gave Mingus the folded envelope, thinking how foolish the men were to go off on such an undertaking with nothing more than the dead man's letter to guide them. The five didn't stand a chance of finding the buried money, in Hob's estimation, but if they wanted to go he wouldn't stop them.

"Be careful, ol' hoss," Hob said when Mingus had the letter in his pocket. "Watch your backsides."

Mingus gave Hob a knowing grin, reaching in his saddlebags for a tiny jelly jar. At first, Hob thought the jar was empty, until a closer look revealed a wilted piece of greenery at the bottom of the jar.

"Takin' my four-leaf clover," Mingus said, as though it settled the issue. "Lady Luck will be ridin' along. No need to worry, partner."

Mingus, Shorty, Soap, Scoop, and Cookie rode off at a trot, following the tracks. Shorty looked over his shoulder and yelled, "You and Tip will get an even share, just the same as if you came with us."

Tip grunted, his eyes on the backs of the departing riders. "Hope they come back in one piece," he said, a remark that added to Hob's worries.

Hob gave Tip a questioning stare.

"There wasn't but one set of tracks," Hob said. "There's five of them."

Tip's dark eyes settled on Hob's face. "One man who knows how to handle himself could give the five of them a fit, Hob. Those men are cowboys. Hardly a one of 'em knows which end of a gun shoots lead."

Hob swallowed hard, turning back to the south. "Those men are my friends. You reckon we should trail along just in case?"

Tip shrugged, eyes to the horizon. "You're the ramrod of this outfit. Me, I'd just as soon be over in Ojinaga drinkin' tequila and peekin' under Rosita's skirt. We've been two weeks sleepin' on hard ground, Hob. If the five of them are fool enough to want to spend their time off looking for buried money, I say we let 'em do it."

"Let's head for Ojinaga," Hob said, agreeing with Tip. "They're grown men, all but Scoop. It's their choosing."

Hob and Tip rode back to the river and made the shallow crossing in silence. Something was eating at Hob, a growing concern over the departure of his cowhands. He decided, after a bit of contemplation, that it was the hanging. Finding Cobb hanged from a tree limb had put a scare into him, since it wasn't a usual way for men to settle their differences. The man who hanged Dave Cobb wasn't an ordinary sort . . . he'd proved it by the way he'd dealt with Cobb.

Tip strung the extra horses together head-and-tail, while Hob harnessed the mules to the chuck wagon. When all the gear was loaded, Hob climbed to the wagon seat and flicked the reins over the backs of the mules. Amid the rattle of harness chains and the creak of axles they were off, aiming west, following the winding course of the Rio Grande. Tip brought up the rear with the saddle string. Before the sun was two hours high, Hob swung the team down a dim pair of wagon ruts that would take them to the river crossing above Ojinaga. Hob settled against the wagon seat, preparing for a long day of travel, knowing it would be well past dark when they reached the little border town.

Driving the team required no concentration, so Hob let his thoughts wander to the five men who rode south into Mexico. He didn't believe Mingus's four-leaf clover offered any protection from bandits and Indians, but he wished his men good luck anyway. If trouble came, Mingus was capable of handling himself in passable fashion, and Soap Osborn was a good shot with a pistol. But Shorty would most likely be drunk as soon as he was out of Hob's eyesight, Cookie Bascom couldn't shoot his way out of a church picnic, and young Scoop wouldn't amount to much if the men were jumped by bandits. Still, there were five of them to back each other's play. Hob decided that it made no sense to worry about them. They'd be all right, he told himself.

The monotonous rattle and creak of the wagon put Hob to sleep in short order, but he was constantly awakening just before he fell off the wagon seat. The country they rode through was empty. The canyons became deeper the farther west they went. To Hob's left lay the river, a muddy expanse of shallows and sandy shoals that seemed to go on forever. Hob put his mind on the night they would spend in the little Mexican village, thinking of the taste of tequila and warm flour tortillas while they listened to the music of the guitars. Once, he caught himself grinning when his thoughts strayed to Carmen and Rosita and the others. It had been better than two months since he'd had a woman. Sitting that lonesome wagon seat, he felt his sap starting to rise.

It was full dark when the wagon crested a hill so Hob could see the twinkling lights of town below the river. Hob slapped the reins to hurry the mules. He could almost taste the first stinging bite of tequila rolling across his tongue.

The wagon made the shallow crossing easily. Hob drove to the tiny livery south of town, where he would tend to the horses and mules before pulling the first cork on a jug of agave juice. Before Hob was down off the wagon seat, Tip rode up to the wagon with a bottle in his fist, offering it to Hob.

"Couldn't wait." Tip grinned. "Have a snort, Hob, an' then we'll see to these animals."

Hob hoisted the bottle and let a mouthful slide down his

dry throat. The burning was like a fire, even when the tequila settled into his belly.

"Mighty tasty, ain't it?" Hob asked, handing the jug back to Tip. "I've worked up a powerful thirst. Let's put these mules away and see if you and me can drink this place plumb dry."

When the animals were stabled, Tip and Hob walked to the big adobe cantina that made up the center of the village. They peered through open windows before they made the batwing doors. Inside, a handful of vaqueros sat around little plank tables, listening to a boy strum softly on a twelve-string guitar. No sooner had Hob and Tip entered the place than a cry came from a corner table. Carmen and Rosita ran toward them, arms outstretched, calling the cowboys' names as though they were greeting old friends.

Rosita flung her arms around Hob's neck, then planted a big wet kiss on his cheek.

"Senor Hob," she cried, smiling, smelling of perfume. Hob's eyes fell to the swell of Rosita's bosom. Her low-cut blouse did little to hide her voluptuous breasts. Long black hair swept her shoulders, tied away from her face by yellow ribbons.

"Tequila!" Tip shouted, his arm around Carmen. "Fetch us another jug and something to eat. Me and Hob aim to have us one hell of a party."

They were shown to a table. Before Hob could pull his chair underneath him, a waiter arrived with a fresh bottle of tequila and a platter of tortillas. Then bowls of chili arrived, still steaming. A swarthy Mexican bartender brought bowls of fresh limes and salt, grinning broadly at his newly arrived customers.

"Welcome to Ojinaga," he said, then his face fell a little when a look toward the door told him that Hob and Tip were alone. "Where are the others?" he asked.

"They'll be along directly," Hob replied as Rosita slid into his lap, smiling with the anticipation of his money. "Maybe tomorrow. Right now it's just me and Tip Giles. We decided to give ourselves a head start. It's been a while."

Tip uncorked the fresh bottle and poured ceremoniously into four shot glasses. Carmen removed Tip's black hat, then wormed her way into his lap. When the glasses were full, they were lifted in a toast. "Here's to luck," Tip said, grinning, then he knocked back his drink.

After they had gulped their drinks, Hob told Rosita, "Soon as I get a bellyful of food, I need a bath. Boil some water for us. Me and Tip will come to the bathhouse shortly."

Rosita giggled, then pecked his cheek with a kiss and motioned to Carmen. Hob watched the two women disappear through a curtain into a room off the back of the cantina, thinking of the pleasure that would follow.

"Let's eat," he said, lifting a spoon as he winked at Tip. "We got our work cut out for us tonight, Tip. No competition from the rest of our bunch, seein' as they're off on a wild-goose chase. We'll have the girls to ourselves."

Hob had eaten until he was sure his skin would pop, and in the process consumed half a bottle of tequila. His legs were a little unsteady as he walked back from the livery carrying his warbag containing a change of clothes.

The main street of Ojinaga was deserted, except for a carriage that rolled into town from the south, pulled by a team of sleek harness horses trotting smartly. In spite of his haste to get to the bathhouse, Hob stopped to stare at the carriage when it went past.

Light from the cantina windows played over the two occupants of the carriage: an elderly man wearing a sombrero, and a much younger woman. The carriage came to a stop. To Hob's surprise, the woman was staring back at him. For a time they simply looked at each other. The old man climbed down from the buggy seat and offered his hand. Only then did the woman look away.

She came down from the carriage as gracefully as a cat,

stepping lightly to the ground in front of the cantina, holding on to the old man's arm. When Hob saw her in better light, he felt something stir inside his chest. She was a dark-eyed Spanish beauty, with creamy complexion and long black hair hanging down her shoulders.

Then she glanced Hob's way again. He flinched and felt his heart flutter. Reminded of his manners, Hob quickly pulled off his hat and gave a courteous bow.

"Evening," he said, thankful for the cover of darkness. He could feel a flush creeping into his face, the way it did when Clara Barclay spoke to him. All his life he'd been uncomfortable around proper women. He lacked experience with them, and he knew it showed.

"Good evening, sir," the woman replied in perfect English.

"Buenas tardes," the old man said, eyeing Hob cautiously. It was his bedraggled appearance, Hob knew, that aroused the man's concerns. He and the men had been camped on the ranch for most of two weeks; he hadn't shaved or been near bathwater, and his clothes looked as if he'd slept in them. He had.

"Glad you ain't downwind from me," Hob stammered, unaccountably saying things he ordinarily wouldn't. "I was on my way to the bathhouse. I look more presentable when I'm cleaned up."

A smile crossed the young woman's face.

"You are a vaquero, senor," she said. "A cowboy does not have to dress elegantly when he is working. Are you from one of the ranches in Texas?"

"Yes, ma'am, I am. The Bar B Ranch . . . Tom Barclay's spread. I'm Hob Shedd, foreman at the Bar B."

It seemed he'd said more just then than he ever had to another woman. Words came tumbling from his mouth.

The woman smiled again.

"I am Elena Montoya," she said, "and this is my father, Don Miguel. Our ranch is south. We are on our way to El Paso to arrange selling our cattle in Texas."

"Pleased to meet you," Hob mumbled, fingering his hat brim, suddenly as edgy as a cat under a rocking chair. When Elena Montoya looked at him, he felt oddly naked. "Are you stayin' the night in Ojinaga?"

"Yes," the old man said quickly, taking his daughter's arm to lead her to the porch of the cantina. "Good night, Senor Shedd. We are very tired after a long day of traveling."

Hob bowed again, but with his eyes still on the woman. To his surprise, Elena also looked at him until she disappeared into the batwing doors.

Hob turned toward the bathhouse, settling his hat back in place. He noticed a strange lightness to his steps and wondered if it was the tequila. At the door to the bathhouse he paused briefly, casting a look over his shoulder.

"Damn, that's a pretty lady," he said, shouldering his warbag before he walked inside.

He found Tip seated in one of the big iron tubs, up to his neck in soapy water. Carmen was bent over him, shaving the whiskers from his face. A half-empty tequila bottle sat beside the tub. The room was filled with the smells of hair tonic and soap. Tip grinned when he heard Hob's spurs jangle across the floor.

"This is the life, Hob." Tip sighed.

Rosita entered the room carrying a steaming bucket. She poured the water in another tub and motioned to Hob.

When Rosita and Carmen left the room, Hob undressed. Fisting a bottle of tequila, he stuck his foot into the hot water and yelped once, then lowered himself into the soapy foam and let out a deep sigh. He rested his head against the back of the tub and closed his eyes briefly, remembering the striking beauty of the woman who had arrived in the carriage and the sound of her voice when she spoke to him outside the cantina. "Elena Montoya," he said dreamily, awakening Tip from a catnap.

"Who?" Tip asked sleepily.

"Elena Montoya," Hob replied. "A real lady. I met her outside a moment ago. Prettiest woman I ever saw, Tip."

Tip grunted and closed his eyes again. "If she's a real lady like you say, she ain't gonna have nothing to do with the likes of you, Hobart Shedd. Real ladies don't associate themselves with common cowboys."

Hob swallowed a mouthful of tequila and stared blankly at the ceiling, considering the possibilty despite Tip's black predictions on the subject.

An hour later, Rosita, Carmen, and the two cowboys sat at a quiet corner table chewing salted limes and drinking tequila. Hob was pleasantly drunk, as was Tip, judging by the difficulty he had pronouncing words. For a time Hob simply enjoyed himself, now and then running a hand underneath Rosita's skirt to feel the softness of her thighs. After several more drinks, the fuzziness in Hob's skull worsened.

At the sound of boots coming through the door, Hob blinked his eyes to get a clear look at a big, barrel-chested gent walking through the batwings.

Beneath a flat brim hat a pair of quick green eyes surveyed the cantina cautiously. When the big cowboy saw Hob and Tip, he started toward them. Hob noticed a .44 on the man's hip.

"Trouble," Tip whispered. Hob saw Tip's gun hand stiffen.

"Howdy, boys," the stranger said, fixing them with a look. It was then that Hob noticed a badge on the stranger's shirtfront. "The name's Carl Tumlinson, Texas Rangers."

Tip's hand relaxed below the tabletop.

"Good idea, cowboy," Tumlinson said, eyeing Tip's hand.

"Just bein' careful," Tip replied. "Didn't see the badge right at first."

Tumlinson stared at them until the silence grew heavy.

"Off your range a bit, ain't you?" Tip asked. "This ain't Texas, in case you didn't know."

The Ranger's face hardened. "Unofficial business," he replied. "Askin' a few questions."

"Ask them." Tip shrugged.

"Take a chair and have a drink with us," Hob said, motioning to the bartender for a clean glass. "What sort of questions are you askin'?"

The Ranger drew back a chair and sat across the table from them. Rosita and Carmen left quickly when the shot glass arrived, whispering to each other and eyeing the badge on Tumlinson's chest.

"Lookin' for some fellers," Tumlinson began. "Texans. They'll stick out like a sore thumb down here. You two are the first white men I've seen since I crossed the river. Let's start off by having the two of you tell me your names, and what you're doing in Mexico."

"I'm Hob Shedd, and this is Tip Giles. We work for Tom Barclay. The Bar B Ranch runs east and north of the river. Good-sized spread. Headquarters is a three-day ride from here."

Hob's foggy brain was clearing quickly. He wondered if the Ranger's visit had anything to do with the man they'd found in the tree.

"I stopped off at the Bar B on my way down," Tumlinson said, nodding thoughtfully. "I had a word with Tom Barclay. He told me he had a branding crew out this way. I reckon you're it."

"Part of it," Hob replied. "The rest will be along in a day or so."

Tumlinson's face was expressionless. He looked from Hob to Tip, working the muscles in his cheeks. "You boys seen anybody pass this way the last few days?"

Hob took a sideways look at Tip, wondering if he should make mention of Dave Cobb. There was something about Carl Tumlinson that made Hob edgy.

"Hadn't seen a living soul," Hob said, which was the truth

in an offhanded way. Cobb was dead when they found him, so it wasn't an outright lie.

"You've got no jurisdiction down here," Tip remarked.

The comment angered Tumlinson. He turned to Tip and set his jaw.

"You're right, cowboy. I'm here anyway."

"Who're you after?" Hob asked softly, trying to appear casual.

The Ranger hesitated, appraising Hob and Tip before he said more.

"Outlaws," he said finally. "Bank robbers. Could be several of 'em. They held up the Cattleman's Bank in Abilene. I've trailed them all over this part of the state. A couple made it to Mexico. There's some who didn't."

Hob found that he was suddenly cold sober. It was the mention of a bank robbery that did it. Now he was certain the Ranger's arrival in Ojinaga was connected to the hanging. Hob wondered if Tumlinson had been the one who hanged Cobb. Maybe that's what he meant by some who didn't make it.

"The Cattleman's Bank," Tip said softly. "When did it happen?"

"Three months back," Tumlinson replied. "It was one hell of a haul. There was a payroll headed for Fort Concho. They got it all. Everything."

"How much?" Hob asked.

"Twenty thousand dollars," Tumlinson said.

Tip whistled softly through his teeth. "No wonder you're goin' to so much trouble," he said.

Hob felt sweat pop out on his forehead. The room felt unusually hot. "Tell us about the ones who didn't make it— you said some got away to Mexico and some didn't."

Tumlinson fixed Hob with a cold stare. "I don't see how that's any of your affair, cowboy," he said. "I do my job."

Tumlinson hoisted his drink and emptied it. Hob took the opportunity to sneak a glance at Tip.

"I reckon I'll be on my way," the Ranger said, pushing his chair back. "You boys keep your eyes peeled. If you happen to see any strangers in these parts, I'd be obliged if you left word here with the barkeep. Thanks for the drink."

Tumlinson stood up. Hob and Tip kept their silence.

"Twenty thousand dollars is a hell of a lot of money," the Ranger said, as though it was an afterthought. "That much . . . it'll be enough to make somebody's tongue start waggin'. I'll hear about it when they start to spend it. Be seeing you boys."

They watched the Ranger until he was out of sight through the doors. It was Hob who spoke first.

"I'll bet a new hat he's the one who hung Cobb."

"Likely," Tip replied, one eye on the doorway. "He so much as said so. Something don't ring true about him, Hob. A Texas Ranger ain't got jurisdiction across the river in Mexico. I say he's acting on his own. Could be he aims to get his hands on that money for himself."

"We're just guessing about the hangin'," Hob replied. "He didn't admit to it. All he said was, there were some who didn't make it to Mexico."

"Mr. Cobb didn't," Tip observed dryly. "I bet Tumlinson caught up with Cobb before he crossed the river, and when Cobb wouldn't tell where the money was buried, Tumlinson hung him to try to make him talk. Cobb didn't tell about that letter, so the Ranger left him at the end of that rope and went looking for the loot on his own. Since he didn't see the letter in Cobb's boot, he don't know exactly where to start."

"Could be," Hob said, thinking on it. "That letter makes it sound like Cobb and his friends knew the whereabouts of that cave before they pulled the robbery. Remember it said Cobb would know the place?"

"They planned their getaway beforehand," Tip suggested.

"Abilene's a hell of a long way," Hob observed. "It would take a week to make the ride," he went on, remembering miserable cattle drives to the railhead in Abilene with Bar B cows.

"If there was twenty thousand dollars at stake," Tip observed, "they could afford the time to plan the job right. I reckon they knew about the big army payroll. Those owlhoots knew the law would come after them hot and heavy, so they planned their escape into Mexico, figuring the law couldn't follow after they'd swum the river. They hadn't figured on a crooked lawman like Tumlinson."

Hob frowned over it while he poured more tequila; then he remembered Mingus and the others.

"Wonder if the boys have found anything?" he asked. "If that Ranger found out they were looking for that loot, I'd say our friends might find themselves in a fix. Tumlinson would be on their trail, especially if he found out about that letter. Without it, Tumlinson don't know where to look."

Tip stared out one of the windows, toying with his glass.

"They could get themselves killed," Tip said.

Hob thought about Tip's remark. Tom Barclay would hold Hob accountable if anything happened to the men. "Maybe Tumlinson will keep his distance. I figure he won't try to tangle with five men carryin' guns."

Tip turned away from the window. "They're cowhands, but Tumlinson is a Ranger. He will be a dangerous man. I've tangled with his kind before."

"There is something about him," Hob agreed, remembering the nervous green eyes and the Colt .44 tied low on the Ranger's leg. "Maybe we ought to ride back and look for Mingus . . . to warn them about this maverick Ranger?"

"Too risky," Tip replied quickly. "Tumlinson might follow our tracks. We'd be leading him straight to Mingus."

"We've got to do something," Hob observed. "We can't just sit here and let Tumlinson make the first move."

"Not much we can do besides wait." Tip sighed. "Mingus and the boys should be here tomorrow night. We can warn them to keep their mouths shut about that letter."

Hob considered another dark possibility. "What if they've found the money?" he asked, whispering.

Tip grinned. "That's about as likely as finding a diamond in a mule's ass, Hob."

Tip poured another round of drinks. Just then Carmen and Rosita came from the back room, smiling as they returned to the table.

"Is trouble?" Rosita asked, glancing toward the door as she slid into Hob's lap again.

"Not for us," Hob replied. "He was asking questions about some outlaws he's after. He ain't after us."

Rosita's face darkened. She glanced at the windows to see if anyone was listening.

"The *Tejano,* he is . . . *malo hombre* . . . a bad one," she said. "He rides his horse to the mountains during the day. All night he watches the streets of Ojinaga, like a cat, as if he is expecting someone."

Hob fidgeted, not from Rosita's weight but from a sudden pang of anxiety. He wondered if Carl Tumlinson was out there now, watching the cantina.

Hob's thoughts were interrupted by the creak of the batwing doors.

Elena Montoya and her father walked in. As soon as they were inside, Elena noticed Hob. She turned toward him, saw Rosita seated upon his lap, and quickly looked the other way.

Damn, Hob thought, wishing Rosita were someplace else just then. Hob marveled at Elena's striking beauty as she accompanied her father to the long wooden bar. Hob noticed that every vaquero in the room was staring at her. Even the young guitar player missed a cord when she first entered the place.

"Mercy," Tip sighed under his breath, looking toward the bar. "Who in tarnation is she?"

Carmen pressed her palm against Tip's cheek, turning his face toward hers.

"She is Doña Elena Montoya," Carmen whispered. "She is the daughter of the richest man in all of Chihuahua, Don

Miguel Montoya. She has no eyes for a poor vaquero, Senor Tip."

Tip grinned and said, "She's damn sure pretty," feigning an effort to turn his face toward the bar where the woman stood beside her father.

Don Miguel bought a bottle of tequila and took his daughter by the arm. When they turned to leave the cantina, Elena's dark eyes flickered toward Hob again. Their eyes met briefly, and just then Hob would have rather been dead. Strangely, before Elena looked away, Hob thought he saw a look of amusement pass over her face. The look was gone before Hob could be sure of it, then Elena walked out of the cantina on her father's arm. Hob's throat was suddenly as dry as sand.

"She was lookin' at you, Hob," Tip said, half hooting. "Saw it for myself. That rich gal has got her eyes on you. Damn if I can figure why, seein' as you're so ugly, but her eyes damn near popped out of her head when she saw you."

Hob swallowed hard, wondering if Tip could be right. It did seem that Elena Montoya was staring at him just then, even though the moment was over in an eyeblink.

Rosita stirred in Hob's lap. When he glanced up at her face, she was smiling.

"Poor Senor Hob," Rosita cried, mocking him with the tone of her voice. "The rich woman teases him. She knows she is beautiful. She is not for you, Senor Hob. She only plays with you."

Suddenly Rosita's fingers were behind Hob's head, pulling his face toward her chest. Before Hob could stop himself, he found his face buried in the soft flesh of Rosita's bosom. He heard Tip's laughter. Rosita giggled.

"There, now," she said. "This will take your mind off the daughter of Don Miguel."

Hob knew he was blushing when he pulled his face back. He laughed, sneaking a sideways glance at the window to be sure Elena wasn't watching from the darkness.

CHAPTER 3

Hob tiptoed quietly through the door and left Rosita's hut, pausing on her front porch long enough to pull on his denims and boots. In the soft light of daybreak his bare legs reminded him of bleached cattle bones, so he hurried to dress himself before anyone else happened by. It was too early for the people of Ojinaga to be about, but Hob was taking no chances. When he had buckled his gunbelt around his waist, he stepped off the tiny porch and set out for a cup of coffee at the cantina. He walked softly toward the dark adobe building, taking great pains not to plant either foot too hard, because the jarring movement made it feel as if someone had dropped an anvil on his head. He was certain that his skull would burst before he'd gone a dozen steps.

"I swear I'll never touch another drop of tequila," he whispered, mincing over the hard caliche ground like a man who was out to steal a sackful of chickens. "Never again," he added hoarsely, as if it were somehow necessary to reaffirm the promise he made to himself.

Hob turned for the back door into the cantina, walking on the balls of his feet. He crept into the kitchen, seeking coffee, considering a platter of eggs. He met a sleepy-eyed cook and grunted a greeting of sorts, searching for a tin cup among the clutter beside a washtub. He poured a shaky cup of coffee from the pot bubbling on the big iron cookstove, trying to stop the trembling in his arms. "Eggs," he said when he noticed that the cook was staring at him. He walked gingerly to the door and entered the main room of the establishment, silently thankful that he was alone in the place. He took a table near a window and eased his body into a chair.

Just as he sat down, he heard the clatter of iron shoes coming down the street. He turned to the window, spotting a lone horse and rider. One look told him the horseman's identity. Carl Tumlinson rode a rangy black gelding down the empty street, cradling a rifle in the crook of his arm. The Ranger's face was hidden beneath his hat brim, but Hob was certain those green eyes would be moving just now, watching everything.

Hob listened to the echo of the horse's hooves until the sound faded, wondering which direction the lawman would ride when he got out of town.

"Hope it ain't east," Hob mumbled, thinking of Mingus and his friends. Right about now, the Bar B cowboys would be riding the canyons searching for the cave and the money. Hob found himself wishing he'd ridden along with the others. He'd be there to lend a hand if trouble came, and he wouldn't have such a splitting headache from so much tequila.

He sipped coffee, worrying about the safety of Mingus and the others in one of the canyons. If Tumlinson rode up on them, Mingus would see the badge and never guess that he had anything to fear from a Texas Ranger. Likely, Mingus would spill his story about the letter and the buried bank loot. Then, if Carl Tumlinson was truly the maverick Hob guessed he was, Mingus and the rest of the bunch would be in real danger. In spite of himself, Hob saw the body of Dave Cobb in his mind's eye, twisting in the breeze at the end of that rope. Hob remembered the way the body turned slowly in the wind, until the dead man's face was turned squarely toward Hob. Only this time, Hob imagined the face belonging to Mingus.

Hob shivered, forcing his thoughts to other things, when he heard boots outside the front door. The doors swung open.

Elena Montoya and her father came into the cantina, and when Elena saw Hob, she smiled.

"Good morning," she said. *"Buenas dias, senor,"* Don Miguel said, but with less enthusiasm than his daughter.

"May we join you for breakfast?" Elena asked.

Her question took Hob by surprise, distracted as he was by her sudden and unexpected appearance in the cantina. This morning Elena was dressed in a brown riding suit, adorned by silver conchos. He stared at her briefly, admiring the outfit and the beauty of her smile, until the dark look Don Miguel gave his daughter reminded Hob of the question she had asked.

"Of course," Hob replied, too quickly, leaving no doubts about his enthusiasm for the idea. Hob pointed toward vacant chairs.

Elena came toward him, smiling sweetly. Hob, suddenly remembering his manners, jumped to his feet and pulled back a chair for her, a movement that rewarded him with a jolt of pain near the base of his skull, a reminder of last night's efforts to drink the town dry.

"Headed for El Paso?" Hob asked, remembering their brief conversation of the previous night.

"Yes," she replied. "We are rested now. The beds at the hotel are very comfortable."

A clapboard building across the street from the cantina served as the town's only sleeping quarters. The place saw very little traffic, since most visitors to Ojinaga were cowboys who spent their nights with the cantina whores in the tiny adobe huts around at the back. The village of Ojinaga was a watering hole on the edge of the Chihuahuan desert, off the main roads into the interior of Mexico. Common travelers were rare.

"You and your father need to keep a sharp eye," Hob said, remembering the empty wastes between the Barclay ranch and the city of El Paso. "That can be dangerous country. This summer we found Indian sign in the south part of the

Davis Mountains. Likely Comanches. Was it me, I'd ride north to Fort Davis and wait 'til they had a patrol headed west. They get wagons full of supplies from El Paso once a month. You could travel back to El Paso with the empty wagons. It'd be safer."

"We appreciate your advice, senor," Don Miguel said softly. "I have made this trip before. I have a rifle."

Hob knew a rifle wouldn't discourage a band of Kwahadie Comanches, but he held his tongue and said nothing. Hob found himself sneaking sideways glances at Elena, admiring the soft lines of her pretty oval face and her big chocolate eyes. When she looked at him he felt an odd weakness in his knees, as if they wouldn't support him if he tried to walk.

The cook sauntered in with Hob's platter of eggs. When she saw Elena and Don Miguel, she hurried over to the table. Hob's plate was dropped in front of him, then the cook asked for their order in Spanish, ignoring Hob.

When the cook departed, Elena smiled at Hob again.

"Where is this ranch you work for?" she asked.

"East, across the river. It's a big spread. The boss man usually runs about two thousand head of mother cows. You and your father should pay Tom Barclay a social call. He and his wife would make you feel welcome. Mr. Barclay, he'll talk horses and cattle until your ears fall off. He'd like nothing better than to have a visit from folks who run cattle down here in Mexico. He'll show off his new bulls, if you're interested. He bought them up at Fort Smith, and they're called Herefords. They cross-up mighty nice on a longhorn cow. The calves have more beef . . . they bring more money up in Abilene."

"Very interesting," Don Miguel replied. "You say they are called . . . Herefords?"

Hob nodded his head. "Wait'll you see 'em. They're pretty to look at, to boot. Bright red, with snow-white faces."

"I think I would like to see these Herefords," Don Miguel

replied, taking a little more interest in Hob. "Perhaps, on our return from El Paso, we will come."

"Mr. Barclay would like that, I'm sure, and so would I," Hob said, realizing when he said it that he'd included himself, a fact that made him suddenly self-conscious, since it was plain it was the woman he looked forward to seeing again. Making matters worse, Elena was looking at him now and she was smiling.

"I would like to visit a big Texas rancho," she said. "Most of the ranchos in Chihuahua are very small."

Hob remembered what Carmen had said about the Montoyas being the richest family in this part of Mexico. "How about your ranch?" Hob asked.

The question seemed to embarrass Elena, and Hob couldn't figure why.

"It is very large," Elena began, "and very lonely. Our house is many miles from Torreon."

The mention of Torreon sent a jolt through Hob. He tried to hide his reaction as he recalled that the outlaw who wrote Dave Cobb's letter had bought a ranch in Torreon.

"Never been to Torreon," Hob said. "Maybe this winter I'll ride down and see the sights. . . . Maybe drop by and see your ranch while I'm there."

Elena's smile widened.

"We would love to have you as our guest, wouldn't we, Papa?" Elena said, glancing toward her father.

Don Miguel seemed less enthusiastic, yet he nodded his head. "Please visit us if you can."

Then Elena's eyes were on Hob again, and they seemed bright with anticipation. Don Miguel made small talk, commenting on the weather, the dry summer and a rancher's concerns about thin grass in the winter. Their food arrived, and they ate in silence. Hob's eggs had gone cold. He hardly noticed, stealing glances at Elena now and then. Often he found her glancing back at him, and when he did, she would give him one of her beguiling smiles.

I think she likes me, Hob thought, filled with wonderment. He tried to be conscious of his table manners, eating slowly, chewing with his mouth closed. When the meal was finished, they sipped coffee until Don Miguel signaled that it was time to leave.

Hob stood up to help Elena from her chair. Don Miguel eyed Hob suspiciously, then took his daughter's arm.

"Good day to you, senor," he said, bowing slightly. "Perhaps we will see you again."

"Yes," Elena said quickly. "Please come to visit us. You must promise us that you will come soon."

Hob could scarcely believe his ears.

"Yes . . . I'll come. Maybe this fall, in a month or two."

Elena smiled, and Hob was certain that her cheeks colored slightly before she turned for the door. Hob followed the pair out on the porch, watching them walk to their buggy, which was tied to a hitchrail in front of the livery and was loaded with luggage. Once, when they neared the carriage, Elena looked over her shoulder at Hob. When she saw him, she waved and smiled.

Hob waved back.

Damn, he thought. *She's about the prettiest woman in the whole world, and damn if she don't seem to like me. Why would such a beautiful woman take a liking to a cowboy? It don't make much sense.*

The buggy rolled past the porch on its way to the river. He stared at the buggy until it dropped out of sight down the riverbank.

"Hobart Shedd," he said aloud, "your luck is changing."

It was two hours past sundown, and Hob was worried. There had been no sign of Mingus and the Bar B cowboys. Hob paced back and forth across the cantina porch, sipping tequila, having forgotten his oath never to touch the stuff again. Tip sat quietly on a bench beside the door, listening to the sounds of the guitar inside. Tip's bottle was already half empty.

"They should have been here by now," Hob said for what seemed the hundredth time. "Something's wrong. I can feel it in my bones."

"Most of the time your damn bones are wrong," Tip observed. It was a common joke among the Bar B hands: Hob tried to predict the weather by the way his joints felt on a particular day, but usually he guessed wrong, a circumstance he blamed on the sudden turnabouts in Texas weather.

"Not this time," Hob said. "The boys should have been here. I told 'em two days. It's that shifty-eyed Ranger. I saw him ride out this morning, and he ain't back either. I figure he's run across Mingus and tricked him into handing over that letter. Mingus wouldn't figure anything was wrong with giving a Texas Ranger the letter. Under the circumstances, neither would I. Mingus ain't the swiftest sort betwixt the ears, and he likely gave Tumlinson that letter without giving it a second thought."

"So?" Tip shrugged. "Tumlinson goes off looking for the cave and Mingus and the boys ride to Ojinaga. No reason for Tumlinson to do them any harm. I'm bettin' all he's after is the money."

"Maybe," Hob replied softly, eyes to the road, searching the darkness for the shapes of horses. "Could be Tumlinson don't want any witnesses to the fact that he has turned thief. Dead men don't talk."

When Tip had nothing more to say Hob resumed his pacing, pausing now and then to look at the moonlit hills beyond the village, listening. He worried about his friends, especially Mingus. They had been working partners on the ranch for half a dozen years, since Mingus first hired on with Tom Barclay. They had paired off with each other right from the start. Hob took a liking to the red-haired, freckle-faced youngster from Arkansas almost from the first day he rode up to the house asking for work. They had become close friends over the years, in spite of their differences. Hob felt a gnawing certainty that his partner was in trouble just now, he could feel it in his bones.

As he waited, Hob thought about Elena Montoya. He remembered her face, the way she looked when she smiled at him. He caught himself imagining what it would be like to kiss her, the way her lips would feel. Right in the midst of his daydreaming, he heard the faint sounds of horseshoes.

He stopped pacing and stared off in the direction of the sound, wondering, hoping it would be the Bar B riders.

Two horsemen came from the east, entering the outskirts of Ojinaga at a trot. Right away Hob recognized one of them, even in the dark. Mingus rode a horse slump-shouldered, as if he was half asleep. When Hob saw Mingus he let out a breath, though he was puzzled by the absence of the others.

Mingus and Cookie rode abreast of the porch and reined down on their sweat-stained horses.

"Where've you been?" Hob asked, glancing behind them, "and where are the others?"

"It's a long story, Hob." Mingus sighed, swinging tiredly from his saddle.

"Are the boys all right?" Hob asked, still looking toward the eastern hills.

"They went crazy on us, Hob. Shorty had a few pints of whiskey in his saddlebags. Him and Soap got to drinkin' and talkin' about finding that money. When it was time for us to head for Ojinaga, they wouldn't come. Said they was gonna stay and look for that cave. Scoop got hisself talked into stayin' too. Weren't his fault—he ain't old enough to have any sense—but Soap and Shorty acted like they caught a dose of the fever. They aim to keep looking for that canyon. I talked 'til I was blue in the face, but they wouldn't listen."

Hob frowned, thinking about what Mingus had just told him.

"Went crazy as a sackful of loons, Hob," Cookie added as

he came stiffly from his saddle to the ground. "They figure to find that bank loot and spend every last cent of it. The kid, he got caught up in all the excitement. The three of them are gonna starve to death out in them canyons. We never did find the right one, but Shorty and Soap swear they'll keep looking 'til doomsday."

Hob remembered Carl Tumlinson just then. The Ranger hadn't come back to Ojinaga at nightfall.

"See anybody else out there?" Hob asked.

"Sure as hell did," Mingus remarked quickly. "There was this feller we seen once, way off on the rim of a canyon. Seemed like he was watchin' us. He just sort of sat there on his bronc, like he was waitin' for us to make the next move. Never did see him again after this morning."

"Tumlinson," Tip said from his seat on the porch, thinking the same as Hob.

"Who?" Mingus asked.

"A Texas Ranger from Abilene," said Tip. "Have you still got that letter in your pocket?"

Mingus shook his head. "Nope. I gave it to Shorty. Wasn't gonna do me an' Cookie any good, so I left it with them."

A sinking feeling entered the pit of Hob's stomach. It was the boy Hob worried about most. Scoop was barely sixteen, a kid orphaned by an Indian attack in the Davis Mountains. Hob remembered the day Scoop rode up to the house on a razor-thin mule, dressed in rags, a whisker away from starving to death, asking for food and a job. Clara Barclay had taken him in and mothered him like he was her own. And Tom had given the boy a job. If Hob remembered right, it had been two years back, and now the kid was off with Soap and Shorty looking for buried money without the slightest idea that a killer was on their trail.

"Got no choice." Hob sighed, knowing what he had to do. Tom Barclay would understand, under the circumstances. "We'll have to go after them, to warn them about Tumlinson. Get a bite to eat and saddle fresh horses."

Mingus was puzzled. He stared at Hob, his face full of questions.

"I'll explain," Hob said. "Hurry all you can, Mingus. We may be too late already."

CHAPTER 4

HOB, Mingus, and Tip rode alongside the wagon as it rattled past the cantina under the crack of Cookie's whip, crossing patches of lantern light cast upon the caliche road from the open windows. Rosita and Carmen stood on the porch waving to the Bar B riders. Hob and Tip returned the wave. Tip clung to a bottle of tequila, nursing it from the back of his sorrel gelding, preparing himself for the trek across ninety miles of rugged mountains and foothills to the ranch head-quarters. While Hob and Mingus went looking for the three missing cowboys, Tip was to accompany Cookie, because it was a ranch rule that no one ever traveled alone if it could be avoided. When the wagon rolled down to the river crossing, Hob rode up beside Tip to say a few parting words. Cookie hauled back on the mules' reins, then handed Mingus two burlap bags filled with supplies.

"Tell Mr. Barclay why we're delayed," Hob said, taking the bottle when Tip offered it. "He'll understand . . . mostly on account of the boy. We'll stay until we find 'em, or until the trail turns cold."

"I'll pass the word along," Tip said, corking the jug when Hob had taken a swallow. "One thing, Hob . . . you mind your backside. I'm betting that Ranger will turn out to be worse'n a rattlesnake if he thinks he's close to that pile of money. Don't take any chances. I've had some experience with the likes of Tumlinson. He'll kill all of you over that bank loot if he gets the opportunity. Sleep with one eye open. Good luck to you, Mr. Shedd."

Hob acknowledged Tip's warning by nodding his head, then Tip and Cookie were on their way across the shallows

38

of the Rio Grande. Hob watched the wagon until it was safely across, then reined his dun to the east and spurred to a trot toward the moonlit hills as Mingus hurried his roan alongside.

"Damn them," Hob muttered when they were clear of Ojinaga, entering barren stretches of caliche and rock dotted with yucca spikes and clumps of cactus.

"Damn who?" Mingus asked, trying to see Hob's face in the shadow of his hat brim.

"Damn that worthless drunk Shorty Stewart and his sorry partner Soap," Hob hissed, clenching his teeth. "Damn them both for gettin' drunk and filling their empty skulls with fool notions, then talking the boy into going along. When I get my hands on Shorty, I'm gonna take a stick of firewood and use it to put knots all over that cowboy's skull, for what he done to that kid. Me, I don't give a fiddler's damn if Shorty and Soap ride plumb to California lookin' for buried money, so long as they do it on their own. If it weren't for Scoop being with them just now, I wouldn't so much as lift a finger to look for them."

Mingus allowed a lengthy silence to pass, waiting for Hob's anger to cool.

"Take it easy on 'em, Hob," he said gently. "It was the whiskey. There's some who call it the devil's brew. You remember, one winter I got myself caught in the clutches of firewater. . . ."

Hob remembered that particular winter all too well, when he and Mingus were snowed in at the line shack above Pinion Springs. They woke up one morning to find themselves trapped in the tiny one-room cabin, surrounded by two feet of windblown snowdrifts. They had a two-month supply of food and whiskey. By the end of the first week, Mingus had consumed his share of the whiskey and started in on Hob's. Hob remembered that Mingus talked day and night, even when Hob threatened to throw Mingus out in the storm so his tongue would freeze.

"I've tried to forget it," Hob said. "Besides, that was different, on account of all that snow. Shorty and Soap ain't got snow for an excuse. I smelled whiskey on them the other day. I should have put a stop to it right then."

"They're our friends," Mingus said, "and if you've got this Texas Ranger figured right, our friends could be in a heap of trouble. I never would have figured a Ranger turning bad, but like you said, twenty thousand dollars is a powerful big pile of money. I suppose it could tempt a man, even a halfway decent feller wearin' a badge."

"It *is* an awful lot of money." Hob sighed.

They pushed their horses through the hills, moving steadily closer to the dark outlines of the mountains. Most often they rode in silence, with Hob brooding over the trouble Soap and Shorty had brought his way. Now and then Mingus would begin some long-winded discussion that required a comment from Hob, but when Hob refused, Mingus gave up and fell silent. Hob's thoughts were elsewhere, trying to guess the whereabouts of the maverick Ranger, wondering if Tumlinson had already found the wandering Bar B cowboys somewhere in the mountains. The Ranger would find their tracks and trail them until he found the men. He would figure things out quickly when he observed three men riding in and out of every empty canyon they came across. It wouldn't take much to guess that the three cowboys were looking for something. The country was too rough to be grazing land—no grass for cows and no water south of the river—so Tumlinson would know the men weren't looking for strays.

"Scoop and the boys will be all right, so long as they can't find that canyon with the spring," Hob declared suddenly, ending many miles of silence.

Mingus did not offer a reply right at first, studying the moonlit slopes. "May not be too awful hard to find the right one," he said later, "since this country is so damn dry. If a feller used his head, he'd follow the first set of deer or javelina tracks he came across. An animal has got to have water, same as a man. If there's a spring, wild-game tracks will lead straight to it. I tried to tell Shorty yesterday that we ought to be lookin' for animal tracks, but he was too damn crazy drunk to listen."

Hob rode in silence, thinking about what Mingus had said, as a plan took shape. They were a full day behind the three men, figuring the time it took for Mingus and Cookie to ride to Ojinaga. Now, if they followed the tracks at sunrise, they were still too far behind to catch up without a sizable amount of luck.

"You've given me an idea," Hob said. "Come sunup, we'll spread out and start looking for game trails, like you said. If we find one, we'll ride it out. Maybe we can find that spring quicker that way and meet up with the boys. Be damned if you didn't have one hell of a good plan, Mr. Strawn. Seems like once or twice a year your brain actually works. If it happened to be light enough just now so I could see, I'd bet a new hat there'd be smoke comin' out your ears from all that powerful thinking."

Dawn found them in the first rocky crags leading toward the slopes. Farther south, the mountains became part of the Sierra Madres range, stretching deep into Mexico. In their path lay miles of barren mountains known as the Chisos, jutting from the floor of the Chihuahuan desert. Hob's worries grew when early sunlight revealed the size of the mountain range in front of them. Three men could simply vanish into thin air in such an expanse of slopes and winding canyons. He realized he was gambling with his men's lives if he and Mingus abandoned the tracks of the Bar B riders, because once Mingus and he struck another direction, they could never find them again.

"It's a long shot," Hob said, standing in his stirrups for a better view of the land ahead of them. "Let's follow the tracks until we come to the spot where you and Cookie left 'em to ride back to Ojinaga, then we can start keepin' our eyes peeled for a game trail or some deer tracks. I've decided your idea makes more sense than anything else, Mingus. If we find that spring mentioned in Cobb's letter, we stand a better chance of being in the right place to help if that Ranger decides to jump the men he's been trailing. Show me where you and Cookie split off from the others."

Mingus frowned.

"Can't say for sure, Hob. All this country looks about the same just now. Up yonder a ways, I reckon. Maybe a little to the south. Our tracks'll be easy to find. Me and Cookie rode straight west, then turned north so we could strike the river when it got dark."

They hit a trot and rode up a gentle slope. Hob kept his eyes to the ground, as he did when he rode the Barclay ranch looking for strays. Reading sign was a necessary skill for cowboys in open country, even the youngest of the men learned it quickly. Back during the days when Indians were a constant menace, a cowboy's life might depend on his ability to see the hoofprint of an unshod Comanche pony. Even now there were roving bands of Kwahadies and Penatekas in the summer, although fewer of late since the army had strengthened its garrison at Fort Davis a few years back.

Two hours past sunup, they found the tracks crossing an ocotillo flat between the slopes. Hob swung down to examine the prints, touching the edges with a fingertip, judging the sharpness. He stood up when his examination was finished, stretching the stiffness from his legs, when his gaze wandered to another set of tracks a few yards away.

"Look here, Mingus," he said, pointing down. Mingus got down from his saddle to study the single set of prints, frowning, as puzzled as Hob by the direction.

"Somebody is backtracking me and Cookie," Mingus finally said.

"Carl Tumlinson," Hob said softly. "Just like I figured. He'll follow these tracks until he finds who made them, then he'll stay out of sight and let our friends lead him to the spot where the money is buried."

"What'll we do, Hob?" Mingus asked, sounding worried.

Hob squinted toward the east, pondering, judging their chances.

"Gamble," he replied after a moment of silence. "Try to get there first, before Tumlinson makes his play."

They climbed tiredly into their saddles and struck a lope, galloping across the smooth flats until the tracks went up a rocky incline. With their eyes glued to the ground, they rode a winding trail toward higher ground, until Mingus signaled a halt and pointed down.

"Here's where me and Cookie split up with them," he said. Hob read the sign quickly. Five horses had made tracks on a patch of powder-dry caliche. Two sets of tracks led west; those would belong to Mingus and Cookie. Three more went southwest. To one side, Hob found the fresher prints of a single horse, and the boot prints of a man who had left his saddle to read the sign closely.

"I'd judge he wasn't more than a couple of hours behind," Hob remarked, sighting along the Ranger's tracks. "Let's ride, Mingus. Look for a game trail, and keep your fingers crossed that we catch them in time."

They were following the hoofprints some time later, unable to find any animal tracks to guide them, when Hob jerked back on his reins and yelled to Mingus. Hob was out of his saddle, kneeling beside a brittle agave plant, when Mingus reached him.

"Look here," Hob exclaimed, tracing his finger over a single hoofprint in the caliche. "Another horse, riding wide of the trail. That makes five, Mingus. Wonder who the hell these tracks belong to?"

Mingus swallowed, taking a quick glance at the mountains around them.

"Gettin' kinda crowded out here, ain't it?" he said.

CHAPTER 5

HOB couldn't shake the uneasy feeling that they were being watched. Huddled around a tiny campfire, he and Mingus examined the dark silhouettes of boulders beyond the firelight, watching shadows for anything that seemed out of place. At nightfall, the mountain air had turned suddenly cold. They held steaming cups of coffee, more for the warmth than for the taste.

All day Hob had worried about the extra set of hoofprints, wondering who else could be riding through these empty mountains. Now he shivered, as much from apprehension as from the falling temperature. The skin down the back of his neck prickled. Sipping coffee, Hob studied every rock and crevice beyond their fire, trying to shake the feeling.

They had wasted four hours, following a javelina's tracks they ran across in midafternoon. The wild pig had grazed aimlessly, then gone north to a tiny pocket of rainwater hidden beneath some boulders in a bend of the dry streambed; here, Hob and Mingus had rested and watered their horses and filled their canteens. Then they had ridden west again until they found this particular spot where they could build a fire beneath a rocky overhang so the flames couldn't be seen.

"Damn the luck," Hob said again, thinking about the time they'd wasted. "Now it's too dark to see. I reckon we can ride due west until sunup, but we'll be ridin' blind. No way to find any deer tracks in the dark."

"I've been wonderin' about those other tracks all day," Mingus said softly. "You said you figured one belonged to that Ranger. Who do you reckon the other feller is?"

44

"Somebody else who knows about that money, I suppose." Hob sighed, thinking. "Who else would be way out here in no man's land following the tracks of a few horses? Maybe it's another one of those bank robbers? Could be they split up after they robbed that bank, to throw off a posse of lawmen. Maybe the one who wrote that letter and his buddy took the money and rode straight for the border while the rest of 'em, including Cobb, led the posse in another direction."

"The owlhoot called Jack, he must've got himself wounded in the holdup," Mingus added thoughtfully, exploring Hob's idea. "He made the ride to the river, but he died from his wound and then Roy buried him. Likely took his share of the loot. He buried Cobb's share in the cave, then he rode down to Torreon and bought himself a fancy ranch. But the letter didn't mention anyone else being in on the robbery."

Hob shrugged. It was all guesswork "Maybe there's another lawman on the trail?" he suggested. "Or a bounty hunter after the reward."

They were silent for several minutes, finishing their coffee while they listened to the night sounds. Off in the distance a coyote barked, then there was an answering call from its mate. When Hob's cup was empty, he stood up to kick dirt on the flames. Mingus was slower coming to his feet. He was still on his haunches when a gunshot exploded from a ledge above them.

A rifle slug whistled past Hob's face, so close he could feel a sudden rush of hot wind before the bullet slammed into the rocks behind him. As the spent lead ricocheted off the rock, Hob dove for the ground, knocking Mingus flat on his back.

"Watch out!" Hob cried, although the warning came much too late.

Their horses snorted and bolted away from the fire, spooked by the roar of the gun. Hob heard hoofbeats and whirled toward the sound. "The horses," he cried. "Get to the horses. . . . I'll cover you!"

Hob jerked his Colt and rolled over on his belly. He fired once without taking aim. The pistol bucked in his fist, and a finger of orange flame spat from the gun barrel. He heard the bullet slam into solid rock somewhere above the ledge where he'd seen the muzzle flash.

Mingus headed toward the horses. Hob knew the gunman would hear the rattle of Mingus's spurs and take a shot at the sound, so he fired again. The roar of the Colt filled his ears, then he heard the whine of a spent slug bouncing harmlessly off the ledge.

"Damn," he whispered, straining to see through the shadows around the ledge. "It must be that damn Ranger. He's found us and he aims to kill us, just like Tip said."

Hob's ears were ringing. His .44/.40 made one hell of a racket when he fired it, dulling his hearing for several minutes. He sighted along the gun barrel and waited, ready to shoot at the first thing that made a move. His heart was beating rapidly from the sudden scare, and his palms were sweating. When he tried to take a deep breath, it felt as if a mule had kicked him in the chest. Off in the distance he heard Mingus chasing the loose horses. *We're as good as dead if we're afoot in these mountains,* he thought.

There was no movement in the shadows on the ledge. Hob swept his gun sights back and forth, ready to squeeze the trigger, but he could find nothing to shoot at except silent slabs of rock. A minute later he relaxed his grip on the gun and tried to calm his jangled nerves. Suddenly, a darker possibility occured to him: the bushwhacker could be moving higher to take a shot at Mingus.

Hob jumped to his feet with one eye toward the ledge, then crept away from the overhang with his Colt aimed in front of him. He heard the rattle of spurs and took off in a run toward the sound, glancing up the slope where the rifleman might be hidden.

He rounded a turn in the ravine and saw Mingus. Mingus was aboard Hob's dun, trotting off in pursuit of his roan. The clatter of horseshoes would draw the bushwhacker's attention, and in the moonlight Mingus made an easy target. He cupped his hand around his mouth to shout a warning to Mingus, but before he could fill his lungs with air there was a bright muzzle flash from the rocks.

The report from the rifle was like a clap of thunder. Hob's arms jerked when he heard the sound, and his legs almost buckled underneath him. He saw Mingus topple from the saddle and fall limply to the ground as the dun galloped away down the ravine.

"No!" Hob cried, filled with blind rage. He whirled toward the muzzle flash and pulled the trigger. The .44/.40 slammed into his palm when the shot rang out. He fired a second time, knowing he had no target, feeling the gun butt jerk in his hand. The whine of bullets against rock echoed through the night. He'd missed both times.

"Show yourself, you son of a bitch!" Hob cried. He did not care that he was making a target of himself just then. All he wanted was one clear shot at the cowardly bushwhacker who had shot Mingus.

The answer to Hob's challenge came swiftly. A shot thundered from the top of the slope and a bullet kicked dirt in front of his boots. Hob lunged to one side, firing as he fell, blinded by the flash of his pistol. He landed on his chest, blinking, unable to see anything but bright light. His finger tightened on the trigger, and he sent a wild shot toward the slope.

"Hob!" Mingus cried, "I've been hit."

Hob turned toward his partner's voice. Mingus lay flat on the ground beside a boulder.

"Stay down!" Hob shouted, aiming at the spot where the shot had been fired. Hob scrambled to his feet quickly and made a run for the protection of nearby rocks. When he was out of the line of fire he crouched down to gather his wits, figuring his next move. If he stayed put too long, the bush-whacker would turn his sights on Mingus to finish the job. Hob knew he had to keep the gunman busy.

"Over here, you backshootin' bastard," Hob cried. "Show your goddamn face and I'll blow it off your neck, you damned backshooter."

Only silence came from the ridge above Hob. Hob's fingers worked nervously around the butt of his Colt, waiting for the Ranger's next move, hoping it would't be a potshot that would kill Mingus. He had to do something to distract Tumlinson before a bullet ended his partner's life.

"I'm comin' up after you, Tumlinson," he shouted, deliberately. Scrambling over loose stones in boots ill-fitted for the task, Hob made his way toward the ridge with his pistol aimed in front of him, ready to make a kill if he saw a movement or heard the slightest sound.

Near the top he was panting, out of breath, unaccustomed to legwork as he was. Hob was near exhaustion when he scrambled to the rim of the ridge, sighting down his gun barrel.

He blinked when he found the ridge deserted. There was no sign of Tumlinson around the spot where the shots had been fired. Hob aimed down the back side of the ridge, peering into the dark chasm below. He saw nothing. Carl Tumlinson had cleared out as soon as Hob started his climb.

"You're a damn coward, Ranger," Hob cried into the darkness, still seething with anger. "You ain't got the guts to face me, Tumlinson."

Silence greeted Hob's ears. He lowered his gun and sat down to catch his breath, his sides heaving from the climb.

Suddenly, he remembered Mingus. He pushed himself to his feet and started down the rock face, hoping his partner's wound wasn't serious. The nearest doctor would be at Fort Davis, better than a hundred and fifty miles away. If Mingus had taken the bullet in the wrong place, he would never survive the ride to the army surgeon's office. If the wound wasn't too bad, Clara Barclay knew enough remedies to pull Mingus through, but the ranch was a rough three or four days away. Either way, if Hob couldn't stop the bleeding, Mingus would die before they could reach help. Silently, Hob wished for good luck as he hurried down the slope.

He ran when he hit level ground, trotting over to the spot where Mingus lay beside the rock. When Hob knelt down beside his partner, he let out a sigh of relief. Mingus was grinning at him in the moonlight.

"How bad is it?" Hob asked quickly, discovering the blood on the front of Mingus's shirt near his shoulder.

"A flesh wound, Hob," Mingus groaned, abandoning his grin when Hob touched the bloodstain. "I can ride. Feels like the bullet went clear through."

He helped Mingus to a sitting position. "Bad news," he said when he saw the back side of the damaged shoulder. "The slug didn't come out. I'll have to cut it out, ol' hoss, or you'll die of the festering. Damn the luck."

"I'd say it was mighty good luck, Hob," Mingus replied. "It ain't hardly more'n a scratch. Get me back to the fire and warm your knife over the flames before you start cuttin' on me. It was that four-leaf clover that done it, Hob. It saved my life just now. I'm gonna make it just fine."

Hob smiled. 'You're tough as boot leather, Mr. Strawn," he said. "That backshootin' Ranger didn't have any idea he was tryin' to kill the toughest cowboy who ever rode the Rio Grande. I'll heat up that knife and you'll hardly feel a thing."

Hob was flooded with relief as he helped Mingus to his feet. The wound was in a good spot: Mingus would survive it if Hob could get the bullet out without too much bleeding. He would need to tear up his clean shirt for bandages, and the bottle of tequila in his saddlebags would clean the wound and help Mingus fight the pain.

Just then Hob remembered the horses. Everything he needed was in his saddlebags tied behind the dun. The first order of business would be to track down their mounts.

"You reckon it was that Texas Ranger who shot me?" Mingus asked as they were hobbling toward the fire, Mingus's arm around Hob's neck for support.

"I'll swear to it with my hand on a stack of Bibles as high as your head," Hob replied quickly, angry all over again when he thought about Tumlinson's ambush.

"Did you see him?" Mingus asked, searching Hob's face.

"Not exactly . . . but I know it was him."

CHAPTER 6

IT was a procedure Hob knew well. He'd removed flint arrowheads and misshapen hunks of lead from various Bar B cowhands over the years. The hardest part was shutting his ears to the pain, for even the toughest man on the place would scream when the red-hot tip of a knife entered his wound. Knowing the man's life depended on removing the bullet made the job a little easier, yet it seemed twice as tough this time since Mingus was his partner.

"Take another slug of that agave squeeze," Hob said, holding his knife above the flames in a gloved hand. "This is liable to hurt some, ol' hoss. We ain't got a choice . . . the bullet's got to come out."

"I know you'll be as gentle as you can," Mingus said. "Get it done as quick as possible. Don't pay any attention if I start to holler. Stick some cotton in your ears."

Hob glanced at his partner's face. In spite of the cold, Mingus had begun to sweat. A pile of bandages lay to one side of the cowboy's bedroll, within easy reach. Hob decided things were about as ready as they'd ever be. The horses were hobbled not far away, just in case. The knife blade sizzled when Hob touched it with a wet fingertip.

"Ready?" Hob asked softly.

"Yeah. Hurry every chance you get, Mr. Shedd." Mingus grinned.

Hob sloshed a generous amount of tequila into the wound. Mingus winced, then he took the glove Hob offered and clamped it between his teeth. He nodded once, as a bronc rider will when he's ready to leave the chute on a bucking horse. Hob poised the knife tip above the bullet hole, hoping

51

the firelight would be enough to let him see the track of the slug, then plunged the blade into the wound. Mingus stiffened. The odor of burning flesh wafted from the hole. Hob sent the knife deeper, peering into the bloody muscle. Mingus let out a muffled scream, and the cords stood out on his neck.

"Damn." Hob sighed, flinching when Mingus screamed again.

He began working the knife tip in tiny circles, until he felt the blade scrape against something hard. "There it is," he said to himself, withdrawing the bloody knife.

He inserted his finger and felt the rough edges of the slug where it was buried in the shoulder muscle. Working slowly, shutting his ears to his partner's pain-ridden cries, he fingered the piece of lead from its resting place and held it in the firelight so Mingus could see. "Got it," he said, then tossed the fragment into the fire. "Hold on a minute longer . . . I've got to stop the bleeding," he said, first pouring more tequila into the wound, then stuffing a piece of cloth into the hole before he started wrapping bandages around Mingus's shoulder.

Mingus's face was bathed in sweat, and he still held the glove tightly between his teeth. "Take it easy now," Hob said, covering Mingus with a blanket when he was done with the bandaging. "Drink more of this tequila and try to get some rest. Come daylight we'll start back to the ranch. Miz Barclay has some healing salve and laudanum. You're gonna make it, partner. The ride home won't be easy, but you'll make it. We'll take it slow."

Mingus nodded that he understood. Hob removed the glove from Mingus's mouth.

"What about Scoop and the rest of 'em?" Mingus asked in a voice that told Hob about the pain.

Hob stared off at the black mountains, listening to the call of a coyote.

"They're on their own," he said softly.

Before the first gray streaks of dawn came to the sky, they were up and having a meager breakfast of dried jerky and coffee. During the meal Hob made a grim discovery; his gun had been empty when he climbed the ridge after the bushwhacker. He'd fired six times and hadn't reloaded. When he challenged Tumlinson on the moonlit ridge, his gun was useless. He told Mingus about what he'd found, speaking in a hoarse voice, knowing he had risked death in a moment of stupid anger.

"It was the four-leaf clover that done it, Hob," Mingus said weakly. His shoulder was swollen to twice its normal size, but Mingus seemed to be in good spirits in spite of the pain. The bleeding had stopped during the night. When Hob applied fresh bandages before breakfast, he found dried blood over the hole.

"I'm glad you brought that good-luck charm along," Hob said to humor his friend as he helped him into his saddle.

They walked their horses, moving toward level ground to lessen the jolting of the ride for Mingus. An hour past sunup they were winding northwest, following a dry wash. When Hob turned back to examine their backtrail, Mingus would give him a lopsided grin.

Hob thought about the kid they were leaving behind, and the danger the three cowboys would face when Carl Tumlinson made his move against them. Hob knew he had no choice, with the shape Mingus was in, but the idea of riding off from it was bothering him just the same.

Toward noon they entered gentler country, leaving the mountains behind. Hob tried to hold a northeasterly direction when the lay of the land allowed it. The going was slower, yet it was easier on Mingus. Later, when they crested a rise in a stretch of hilly brushland, Hob saw the distant line of deeper green that marked the Rio Grande. They halted on the rise, where Hob climbed down to give the horses the last of their grain in one of the burlap bags. Mingus rested in his saddle while the horses ate, clinging to his saddle horn with white-knuckled hands. Hob knew his friend was growing weaker. Mingus's face was turning red with the fever from his wound. Hob knew tomorrow's ride would be the hardest, when the fever would be at its worst. There was a chance he'd have to tie Mingus across his saddle until the fever broke.

"We'll make the river before nightfall," Hob said. "We can spend the night in Texas on Barclay land."

Mingus nodded and tried for a grin.

"I'll make it, Hob. Don't fret over me."

Hob swung into the saddle and gathered his reins.

"Never doubted it for a minute, ol' hoss," he said. "It's that four-leaf clover, bringin' us nothing but the best for the ride home."

They rode off the rise, aiming for the river. Without a landmark he could recognize, Hob decided to ride the riverbank until the next morning, when they could swing north to look for the wagon road that would take them to the ranch headquarters. The going would be easier.

To pass some time he thought about Elena Montoya again, allowing his mind to wander back to their meeting in Ojinaga and the promise he made to visit the Montoya Rancho when the work was done in the fall. Too, he remembered Don Miguel's vague mention that they might visit the Bar B on their return trip from El Paso. Hob found himself looking forward to it, as remote as the possibility was. He knew he would make the ride down toward Torreon when cold weather set in, just for the chance to see Elena's beautiful smile and to feel the flutter of excitement in his chest when she spoke to him.

Hob could not keep his mind off Scoop. The boy could wind up paying dearly for the mistake of riding off with Soap and Shorty in search of buried treasure. Hob's hands tightened on his reins when he thought about the backshooting Ranger prowling the canyons behind the Bar B men. And there was the fifth set of tracks to wonder about.

With time on his hands, he pondered the mystery of the additional tracks until they rode to the edge of the river. Mingus had begun to sway back and forth in his saddle and Hob knew they would have to rest soon, before Mingus fell from his horse. When they rode into the shallows, the horses drank their fill while Hob kept an eye on Mingus. His partner clung resolutely to the saddlehorn, and his face wasn't the right color.

"You okay?" Hob asked gently.

"Gettin' a mite weak, ol' hoss, but if you'll hand me that tequila I reckon I can make it 'til dark on this rough-gaited roan."

Hob fished the bottle from his saddlebags and gave it to Mingus. Mingus took a few swallows, wincing when he lifted the jug to his lips.

"Maybe I oughta lie down for a spell," he said as Hob returned the bottle to his gear. "Hate to admit it, partner, but I'm about done in. Just let me rest a couple of hours and I'll be able to ride the rest of the night."

Hob could hear the pain behind Mingus's voice, but they pushed on. They crossed water, belly-deep for the horses, and rode out on the Texas side. Once, Mingus tilted dangerously from the seat of his saddle and Hob caught his arm before he fell. When they reached a stand of trees Hob helped Mingus to the ground, then to the base of the largest cottonwood trunk. The cowboy's face was white as Hob quickly spread his bedroll. Almost before his head was against his saddle, Mingus closed his eyes. Half a minute later, he was snoring.

Hob sat beside him for a time, sipping tequila, worrying over the condition of his friend. The toughest test would come tomorrow, and the day after, crossing the Christmas Mountain range and then to the foothills of the Santiagos. It was some of the roughest country in Texas, and in late

summer, some of the driest. If Mingus couldn't ride, he
would have to make the trip tied across his saddle. The
prospects were gloomy. Looking at Mingus just now, his
badly swollen shoulder, his body wracked by fever, Hob knew
the odds were stacking up against him. Rest was what the
cowboy needed most, and time for his swelling to go down.

"Backshootin' bastard," Hob growled, thinking about the
Ranger. "It takes a sorry son of a bitch to bushwhack someone in the dark. He has the gall to call himself a lawman."

Hob stared at the river, watching the ebb and flow of the
current until his anger cooled. He drank tequila. Later, he
got up and hobbled the horses on a grassy flat beside the
river, then built a fire, circling it with stones. He filled the
little coffeepot and put beans on to boil, always with an eye
toward the southern horizon. Down there somewhere in the
mountains of Mexico, his friends were being stalked by a
money-crazed Texas Ranger who had forgotten his oath to
uphold the law. When Hob thought about the peril his men
were in, his hands would ball into angry fists. Looking at
Mingus, Hob wondered if sixteen-year-old Scoop Singleton
had already met the same fate, downed by a dry-gulcher's
bullet.

"Damn," Hob whispered, listening to the soft bubbling of
the coffeepot. "Damn you, Tumlinson."

It was midnight, by Hob's guess, when Mingus started
having difficulty breathing. When Hob touched his partner's
forehead, it felt as hot as a branding iron. "Wake up," Hob
cried softly. "I've got to cool you down, or you'll melt like
snow in July. Open your eyes, Mingus."

Hob shook him. Mingus wouldn't wake up. Hob removed
a spare shirt from Mingus's gear and soaked it in the river,
then wiped the cool cloth over Mingus's face and arms. Over
and over again Hob soaked the shirt and applied it to the
sleeping man's face, with no result. Mingus struggled to
catch each breath, as though he was choking on something.

Hob knew that something had gone wrong inside the damaged shoulder. The swelling had grown even worse, and now Mingus was strangling.

Hob built up the fire so he could see, then undressed the wound carefully. Red streaks ran from the bullet hole, just under the skin. "Blood poisoning," Hob muttered. He'd seen it once before, when Chick Laster took a Comanche arrow in his leg. The wound had been slow to heal, and as a result bright red streaks began to appear near it. Chick had almost died; Clara Barclay had nursed him back to health. But try as he might, Hob couldn't recall what Clara had done to pull Chick through.

Hob poured more tequila into the wound. The flesh around the bullet hole had begun to smell rotten. "Wake up, Mingus," Hob said. "Remember that four-leaf clover, ol' hoss. Don't give up on me, damn it all. Open your eyes and breathe regular."

It was useless; Mingus couldn't awaken from his fevered sleep. Hob continued to soak the shirt in the river and wipe Mingus's forehead. While he was about the task, Hob's fears grew. In the flickering firelight, Mingus had the look of a man who was near death.

"Please don't die on me, partner," Hob whispered, feeling tears come to his eyes when he spoke. "We've been friends a long time now. Don't pull out on me."

They had become friends at once, almost from the first day Mingus hired on at the Bar B. The lanky cowboy had ridden in one afternoon, covered by a layer of chalky dust, asking to water his foot-sore bronc. Hob was a green foreman then, six years back, and when Mingus gave his name Hob asked him to repeat it again, odd as the name was. Then Mingus asked about day work, and Hob wasn't exactly sure how to go about hiring a new man. They needed a couple of cowboys for the roundup and the drive to the railhead, and Mingus had the look of a good cowhand. Hob told him to toss his gear in the bunkhouse, and when Mingus grinned through the layer of caliche dust, Hob burst out laughing at the sight of it. "Take a bath soon as you can," Hob had said, holding his sides, "so I'll be able to recognize you on payday." It was the beginning of a friendship.

Mingus had quickly proven to be one of the best cowhands on the place with a lariat. They became partners for the winter months spent in a line shack. And by the end of the first year, Mingus was his trusted right hand. In the years since, they had ridden countless miles together, listened to each other's tall tales and jokes, talked about a cowboy's dreams for the future, and even shared secrets about women. Hob had never really opened up to any other man before, not even during the war, when every single day was filled with the fear of dying.

It wasn't that Mingus was like Hob at all; in fact, they were two very different types. Mingus was reckless where Hob was cautious. Mingus was as long-winded as any man Hob had ever known, whereas Hob was usually quiet. Mingus could talk a blue streak on most any subject, and he seemed to have an opinion on everything. Most of the days they spent together were conducted in the same fashion: Mingus doing the talking and Hob doing the listening. Hob pretended to be annoyed by it, this constant chatter, when in fact he enjoyed the never-ending stories. It made the days a little shorter and the cowboy existence a little less lonely when they rode the empty land.

Now, as Hob sat beside Mingus just before dawn, he placed his hand on his friend's forearm.

"Stay with me a little while longer, ol' hoss," he whispered. "It'll be lonesome out here without you."

Almost at once, Mingus let out a sigh. The change startled Hob, until Mingus inhaled and his breathing became regular. It was as if he'd heard Hob's request.

At sunup Hob could see the red streaks clearly; they ran across Mingus's chest and down his left arm, radiating from the wound. Hob frowned, wondering what he should do. The scent of rotten flesh had grown stronger during the night. Peering into the bullet hole, he could see traces of yellow pus. In spite of the heated knife blade, the wound was festering.

"I reckon it's like curing the rot in an injured cow," Hob said. "A red-hot iron will burn out the rot so it don't spread. Damn, it'll be hard to put an iron on Mingus. He'll holler like a pig stuck under a gate, but I reckon it has to be done."

He searched his saddlebags until he found the little iron poker, then placed it in the coals and added wood to the fire. He made another pot of coffee and waited until the iron glowed red in his gloved hand.

"I hate doing this worse'n anything on earth," he said, even though Mingus could not hear him. He straddled his partner's chest, wincing when he thought about what the poker would do to the muscle. "Hang on, Mingus." He sighed softly.

He thrust the iron into the wound. In the same instant, Mingus's eyes flew open. He stiffened underneath Hob and then a sound came from his chest, shattering the silence. Downstream, the horses snorted in alarm, startled by the noise.

Hob gritted his teeth, fighting to hold the rod in place while Mingus struggled underneath him. The stench of burning flesh filled Hob's nostrils. Tears came to Hob's eyes again when he glanced into his partner's face.

Mingus gasped, arching his back to rid himself of Hob's weight. His eyes were glazed, and he tried to focus on Hob.

When he could stand it no longer, Hob pulled the sizzling rod from the bullet hole. Mingus fell back against his saddle, unconscious.

"Sorry, partner," Hob said, strangling on the words. "It had to be done. Weren't no other way."

CHAPTER 7

IT was noon before Hob made the decision to carry Mingus down to the river. His fever had worsened, until he became delirious and started mumbling incoherently, though his eyes remained shut. Hob had to do something to lower the fever; the water-soaked shirt was not enough, and he had no medicines with him.

He lifted Mingus in his arms and walked down to the edge of the river. He lowered Mingus into the cool water and held his face above the surface. The sleeping cowboy stirred and groaned once, batting his eyelids. His eyes were glazed over, unseeing, staring blankly at the sky. Then they closed and a long, shuddering breath left him, whispering through his nostrils.

"Please spare him, Lord," Hob prayed, looking toward the heavens. "He ain't never been much of a churchgoer, seein' as we ain't got us a church close by, and the nearest thing we've got for a preacher is Tip Giles reading to us from the Good Book sometimes, so I can testify that Mingus has been exposed to the word of the Almighty, even if it did come from Tip Giles' mouth, which ain't sayin' much. Mingus, I've heard him pray out loud on more'n one occasion, so I know he has tried to stay in contact with You from time to time. I'll swear he's a good feller, if my testimony carries any weight. Now, there've been times when Mingus has been known to cuss, maybe more than his fair share, but he don't mean a thing by it. It's just his way to let loose when things don't go to suit him. But spare his life, Lord—if You judge a man by the goodness inside him, this cowboy is better'n most."

It wasn't Hob's nature to pray unless things were serious;

60

he figured God was too busy to be bothered with trivial matters. Once, when Hob's boot got stuck in a stirrup when a bronc colt bucked him over its head, Hob prayed as loud as he knew how as the horse dragged him down a rocky hillside. Suddenly, his boot came off and he was spared from certain death. Since then, he had firmly believed in the power of prayer, although he saved it for special circumstances. Now and then, when he was alone on the ranch, he would have a talk with God about this or that, mostly dry weather and the need for rain. Apparently, God wasn't quite as concerned about Texas weather as he had been in letting go of Hob's boot, since it seldom rained when Hob asked. But just now, as Mingus lay near death in Hob's arms, Hob felt that the occasion warranted some divine intervention. Mingus couldn't seem to shake the fever on his own.

Half an hour later, when Mingus's color seemed better, Hob carried him up the riverbank to his bedroll. Mingus groaned when Hob put him down, then his eyes opened.

"Where am I?" Mingus croaked. "Is that you, Hob?"

"Yeah, it's me. You've got a touch of the fever, so we're still camped beside the river. Your wound is festered. Somehow, I've got to get you back to the ranch so Miz Barclay can fix you up with her medicines."

Mingus nodded as though he understood. "Put me on my horse. I can make it. If I can't sit a saddle, stretch me over it and I'll be just fine."

Hob swallowed, thinking how hard such a ride would be for an injured man. "It'll be rough," he said softly.

Mingus grinned, his first since Hob put the knife in his shoulder. "I can make it, partner. Let's get started before my left arm rots plumb off. I need that arm to play the fiddle."

Hob laughed, partly from relief. Mingus seemed his old self again. "Wouldn't want anything to put a stop to such pretty music, Mr. Strawn. Some say your fiddle playin' reminds 'em of the sound of a rusted windmill in a high wind, but I've always argued that yours was some of the best dancin' music I ever heard. Some folks just ain't got an ear for good fiddlin' at all."

Hob stood up and dusted off his knees. "I'll go fetch the horses," he said.

Hob halted the dun to study the ground, feeling his heartbeat quicken. He counted the tracks of more than a dozen unshod ponies. It was the worst news he could imagine, under the circumstances. With an injured man who could barely sit a horse, the last thing they needed was an encounter with Comanches. Hob followed the tracks with his eyes. The Indians were moving north into the Christmas Mountains. The tracks were only a few hours old. There were no marks of travois poles, so he could conclude no women were with the warriors. A hunting party, if he was lucky. Or a band of raiding horse thieves, if he wasn't.

"Likely Comanch'," Mingus said, slumped over in his saddle. The cowboy's face was pale and his eyes had sunk farther back into his skull, in Hob's opinion. The ride since noon had taken its toll on Mingus, even when they held the horses to a walk.

"Like as not," Hob agreed, sighting the horizon. "It'll be dark soon. Maybe we won't run across them. Can you still ride?"

"Feelin' better every step of the way," Mingus replied. His voice betrayed him. As always, he was trying to carry his share of the load without being a burden on Hob.

"Take another snort of this tequila," Hob said, offering the bottle. Only a few precious inches of liquid remained, not nearly enough to deaden the pain in Mingus's shoulder all the way to the Barclay ranch.

"I'm liable to get drunk, Hob. Can't help fight them Comanch' if I'm too damn drunk to see straight. Save it for later."

Hob secured the bottle in his warbag and touched a spur to the dun, leading off down the wagon road twisting toward the dim outlines of the mountains. From the looks of things, with a band of Comanches on the prowl, it promised to be a long night.

No rifles, Hob thought, considering the prospects of a fight with the Indians. *We could lose our hair if we get ourselves cornered, and we can't outrun them . . . Mingus can't ride well enough if we get in a hurry.*

A black mood came over Hob. After all they'd been through with the bushwhacking and Mingus's fever, now they faced a band of roving Comanches. It had been Hob's experience that bad luck came in streaks, and their present circumstances tended to support his belief. "It's that damn letter," he muttered under his breath. "Started the whole goddamn thing, it did."

At full dark they rode cautiously to the top of each rise before they continued down the wagon ruts. Hob would sit and take a careful look at their surroundings, listening to every sound, examining every shadow before riding farther. Comanches were a subject he knew a thing or two about, and he feared them more than anything else on earth. As a boy he had spent a few years living among them, helping his father with a meager fur-trading business with the eastern Comanches. The Noconas were the most peaceful of the five Comanche tribes, accepting the white man for the most part, welcoming trade. Young Hob Shedd had learned their language, enough to get by, and learned a thing or two about their ways. It was the western bands that white men feared most, the bloodthirsty Kwahadies and the Kotsotekas. Hob knew the tracks they had found earlier in the day most likely belonged to a party of Kwahadies. A knot formed in his belly when he thought about them: he'd seen their handiwork before, the mutilated corpses they left behind when they fought their enemies.

At night, the air was cooler. And as they rode higher into the Christmas range, a cold wind swept down from the barren peaks. Soon Hob was shivering inside his thin shirt. His guess was the cold would help keep Mingus's fever down.

Hours later, when they came to a stand of scrub live oak beside the road, Hob dismounted and helped Mingus from his saddle, then to a resting place against a live oak trunk. After the horses were hidden in the trees, Hob and Mingus ate jerky and sipped water from their canteens. With Indians riding somewhere in these mountains, Hob wouldn't risk even the smallest fire to boil coffee. He prowled the edges of the thicket while Mingus drank a few swallows of tequila, always listening for any change in the night sounds or the footfall of an unshod pony. Soon Mingus was alseep on his bedroll, exhausted by the ride. Hob found a position near the horses where he sat in the shadow of a tree, dozing now and then until dawn.

"Can't make coffee," Hob told Mingus, staring off at the jagged outlines of the mountains, now bathed in soft golden light. "Makin' a fire would be like inviting every Comanche within three or four miles to a scalpin' party."

Mingus sat up, testing his sore shoulder with his fingertips.

"I reckon I'd rather have tequila anyways," he said, wincing when his fingers touched his wound. "Best news is, my fever broke some last night. I woke up in a powerful sweat. I feel a sight better than yesterday."

They were saddled and moving before the sun cleared the horizon, staying off the skyline until Hob was certain no Comanches were in front of them. As far as he could see, there were only empty mountains and valleys, yet he was still edgy as they rode northeast along the wagon ruts. Experience had taught him one thing about Comanches: they were found where you least expected them.

Midmorning found them in steep climbs through mountain passes. They were riding familiar range now, nearing some of the best high-country pastures for summer grazing, where they had branded calves only two weeks earlier. Hob had begun to relax, since they'd seen no more Indian sign.

Around noon, as they crossed a barren ridge, a sixth sense made him look over his shoulder.

Coming from the north, he saw a sight that curdled his blood. A line of slender mustang ponies trotted from a crag between a pair of rocky peaks. Perched atop each pony was a warrior. Hob knew at once, by the twin braids of hair and pairs of eagle feathers hung down a shoulder, they were Comanches. Only a few white men got close enough to recognize them and then live to tell about it.

"Comanches!" Mingus cried.

Hob looked south for an escape route. Below the ridge they were traveling lay half a mile of switchbacks littered with loose rocks and boulders, the worst possible footing for a running horse. One misstep would mean a shattered foreleg and a certain fate at the hands of the Comanches.

"Ride!" Hob shouted, spurring east along the wagon road. Their only hope lay in following the ruts, giving their mounts better footing with the hope of putting some distance between themselves and the wiry little ponies. The Indians would try to cut them off before Hob and Mingus could reach the next mountain pass. It would come down to a test of horseflesh.

Mingus spurred his roan alongside Hob. "Here they come," he cried, looking over his shoulder. "Sweet Jesus . . . just listen to 'em scream!"

Hob heard the chilling war cries above the clatter of horseshoes. Gooseflesh pimpled down his back. They were in a race for their lives.

He took little comfort in the knowledge that Tom Barclay believed in owning good horses. The geldings they rode were the result of a cross with a Thoroughbred Remount stallion on mustang mares. They had stamina and speed for long distances, but the dun and the roan had been ridden too hard in the weeks since the branding started. Hob's dun wouldn't have much left, and Mingus's roan looked to be in even worse shape. If the Comanche ponies were fresh, the

race would be over soon and he and Mingus would be in a
fight to save their skins, armed only with pistols and a
handful of ammunition. Damn lousy odds, he thought
quickly.

Hob looked back. The Comanches were gaining ground,
bending low over their ponies' necks. A rifle glistened in the
sun in a warrior's hand. Hob took a quick tally of the Indians.
Seventeen were closing the distance, racing their ponies
recklessly over rough, uneven slopes. At least four carried
rifles. Before Hob turned back to watch the road, he saw
something else he recognized: the bobbed tails that marked
the ponies as belonging to a band of Comanches called
Yamparikas. He wondered why they were so far from their
home range.

"Yamps," he cried, looking over at Mingus. "Ain't quite so
bad as I figured. If we can find the right spot, maybe we can
stand 'em off."

Mingus's face twisted with pain as his roan galloped beside
Hob. He couldn't take the jolting of a hell-for-leather ride
much longer. Hob knew they'd have to find cover soon.

A mile farther, their horses were laboring for each breath,
shortening their strides. Hob turned back again. The Indians
were behind them now, following the same ruts. Less than a
quarter-mile stood between them. The ponies were gaining.

Hob noticed a change in the rhythm of the dun's strides as
they neared a narrow pass between two bald mountains. Air
whistled through the gelding's muzzle, warning that the end
was near. Hob judged the distance to the pass, wondering if
his horse stood any chances of making the safety of the
rocks.

"We've got to find some cover," he shouted. "Look for a
place where our horses won't be in the line of fire."

The first sharp crack of a rifle echoed behind them. Hob
whirled in the saddle, measuring the range. With a little
luck, they might make the pass before a bullet found them.
Hob drove his spurs into the dun's ribs, asking the horse for

everything it had. The gelding grunted and lengthened its strides, catching up with Mingus's roan. Hob pulled his Colt and turned back to fire a warning shot, shouting, "Spur like hell for that pass."

He raised his gun sights to take aim at the lead warrior, then he saw a puff of smoke from an Indian's rifle. Suddenly, the dun faltered, shuddering before it went down in mid-stride, crashing to the ground on its chest.

Hob was thrown skyward, as if he'd sprouted wings. His pistol flew from his hand, then he went tumbling, landing in a ball, arms and legs askew. He rolled over on his back and lay still, trying to catch his breath. It happened so suddenly that Hob wasn't quite sure what had caused his fall.

He raised his head, blinking dust from his eyes, when he heard the thunder of running horses and the shrill cries of the Comanches. He turned toward the sound and blinked again.

The charging Indians now formed an uneven line, racing toward Hob. Still stunned by his fall, Hob tried to scramble to his feet, searching the ground around him for his pistol. He was barely able to stand, reeling to keep his feet underneath him, when he heard Mingus shouting behind him.

"Swing up behind me!" Mingus cried, galloping his roan back toward Hob. Hob saw a gun in his partner's fist. Mingus fired once before he reached Hob, reining his horse in a tight circle so Hob could swing up behind the saddle.

Gunshots echoed all around them as Mingus spurred the lathered roan toward the pass. Bullets whistled past, high and wide of their mark. Hob clung to his partner's back, still dizzy from the fall. The roan lunged, reaching a full gallop in three long strides under the punishment of Mingus's spurs. Hob could hear the yipping cries of the warriors, much closer now, and the thunder of the ponies' hooves.

Suddenly, the roan slid to a stop. Hob saw boulders and big slabs of rock around him. He dropped quickly from the roan's rump as Mingus handed him the pistol. Hob whirled and raised the gun, aiming for the closest warrior. The Colt exploded in his hand when he squeezed the trigger, and the Indian spun crazily from the back of his pony.

"Get down, Hob!" Mingus cried, off the roan now, pulling the horse toward the protection of the rocks.

Hob stumbled, aiming for the nearest rock pile in a loop-legged run as he brought his sights to bear on another Comanche. A rifle banged from the line of oncoming warriors, and Hob felt the hot breath of the bullet near his ear. He sighted in on a warrior's chest and squeezed. Hob was falling toward the ground when he saw the Indian roll off the rump of his racing pony, landing under the flying hooves of the ponies behind him in a cloud of yellow dust.

Hob fell behind a rock and peered over it, swinging his sights, then squeezing off a shot. A warrior aboard a pinto pony slumped against the pony's withers. Blood streamed from a wound in the Indian's side; he dropped his rifle to clutch his injury just before he fell, disappearing in the cloud of dust.

"Watch out, Hob!" Mingus cried. A lone warrior had ridden around the pile of boulders, taking aim at Hob with his rifle. Hob whirled and fired. The Comanche's face exploded in a shower of blood before he toppled off the rump of his galloping pony.

The Indians were upon them when Hob fired the next shot at close range. A willowy Comanche boy flew off the back of his mount, tossing his bow in the air before he went out of sight in the melee. Then Hob found another target and pulled the trigger. The hammer fell on a spent cartridge as a line of mounted warriors swept past the rocks where Hob lay.

He ducked down and worked the ejection rod as quickly as he could, fumbling in his haste. He fingered fresh loads from the cartridge loops in his gunbelt and thumbed a handful into place, scattering shells around his boots when they fell from his trembling fingers. Just then he wished for a way to get the other pistol, so Mingus could add to the fire. His .44/40 lay somewhere in front of the rock pile, as useless as teats on a boar hog.

"Nice shootin'," Mingus shouted, hunkered down behind a boulder, clinging to the roan's reins.

Hob peered above the rocks again and pulled the trigger when a warrior filled his sights. He'd done it too quickly, and the shot was wide. Muttering under his breath, he cussed his bad luck and sought a new target.

Two quick shots felled two more warriors. He watched one land disjointedly in the dirt, dead before he hit the ground from a bullet through his head. "Lucky shot," he told himself. He had aimed for the warrior's chest.

The last of the Comanches galloped past their hiding place in a cloud of caliche dust. Hob watched the others circle, just out of pistol range, preparing for another charge.

"Where's my gun?" Hob asked, blinking dust from his eyes.

"Cover me!" Mingus shouted, and before Hob could voice protest, Mingus was off at a run across the battlefield, crouching down.

"Come back!" Hob cried, glancing toward the Indians. One warrior saw Mingus leave the protection of the rocks and heeled his pony after Mingus, screaming a war cry.

Hob drew a bead on the warrior and waited. The fleet-footed pony charged toward Mingus. When the Indian was in range, Hob squeezed gently on the trigger. The Comanche flipped off the rump of his pony with his war cry still echoing from the rocks.

Mingus grabbed Hob's pistol and then made a dash for the pile of boulders. The Comaches formed a ragged line when they charged after Mingus, yipping like coyotes, firing rifles and arrows as they came. Hob laid down rapid fire until his pistol clicked empty, but Mingus had made the boulders and begun firing into the Indians. His aim was bad, but it gave Hob enough time to reload.

CHAPTER 8

AFTER the second wave of attacking warriors swept past their hiding place, Hob took stock of his surroundings. They were in a pocket protected by boulders that had fallen from a steep slope behind them. The spot offered good natural defense against bullets and arrows. The Comanches would have a tough time rooting Hob and Mingus out of the rocks as long as their ammunition held out.

Hob counted nine warriors milling about near the entrance to the pass. Only two carried rifles. The Indians gathered to hold a talk about their next move, giving Hob and Mingus a moment's rest.

"I owe you my life, partner," Hob said, panting, still out of breath from the fall. "If we get out of this scrape with our hair, I'll buy the first round of drinks in Ojinaga."

Mingus was seated beside a rock, thumbing fresh shells into Hob's Colt, trying to catch his wind after the run to retrieve the pistol.

"It wasn't so awful much, Hob," Mingus sighed. "To tell the honest truth, I was just plain scared to face those redskins without you."

It was then that Hob noticed fresh blood on Mingus's shirt.

"Your shoulder," Hob said. "It's bleedin' again."

Mingus nodded. "Hurts something terrible. Right now I'm as dizzy as a dance-hall whore doin' the waltz."

Hob turned his attention to the Indians when he heard a sound. A wounded warrior was crawling away from the spot where he'd fallen from his pony, leaving a trail of blood. "How many shells have you got?" he asked as he considered putting a bullet into the wounded man.

"Hardly a dozen," Mingus replied weakly, slumped against the rock. When Hob looked at his partner, his face was the color of snow. The bleeding was robbing Mingus of his strength. Hob figured it was the run to pick up the pistol that had broken open his wound again.

Hob squinted at the mounted warriors. Losing so many of their number had taken some of the fight out of them. He was thankful again that the Comanches were Yamps and not Kwahadies. The tide might not have been turned so easily had that not been so.

Hob counted the cartridges in his belt loops: just five fresh loads remained, and six in the gun. He was wondering if Mingus carried any more shells in his saddlebags when he heard a cry from the mouth of the pass. One warrior raised his rifle over his head, shouting at the white men. Hob could make out a few of the words.

"What'd he say?" Mingus asked, peering above the rocks.

"They're tryin' to goad us into coming out to fight them," Hob replied softly. "He says we're cowards, hiding behind these rocks."

"He's right," Mingus said, without intending any humor. "Maybe he can't count. There's just two of us."

Hob watched the nine Comanches, trying to guess their next move. With only two rifles, they weren't as likely to make another all-out charge. They seemed content to yell insults and wait to see what the white men would do.

When Hob added things up, he didn't like the tally. They had just one horse and precious little ammunition. Their food was tied behind Hob's dun, lying better than a hundred yards from the rocks. It would be too risky to make a try for the food in daylight; the Comanches with rifles would cut him down. One canteen hung from Mingus's saddle, enough to keep two men alive for three or four days at best.

"If they aim to wait us out, we could be in a peck of trouble," Hob observed. "Our jerky is behind my saddle, and we've got just one canteen. Things don't look much better if they pull out and leave us alone, Mr. Strawn. We've got one horse between us, and we're still two days from the ranch. One of us will be given the opportunity to walk back home, and I reckon the job falls to me, seein' as how you're hurt. Either way it goes, we ain't exactly in the best of shape."

"Could be worse," Mingus said, holding one hand over his wound to stem the bleeding. "We could both be dead back there someplace."

Hob grunted, making a sour face. "I reckon you'll lay claim to all this good luck bein' the result of that four-leaf clover. Me, I ain't quite so inclined to call this predicament good luck. Ever since we found that letter in Dave Cobb's boot, things have gone bad for this outfit. Scoop and Shorty and Soap are liable to be dead already if that maverick Ranger has made his play, and you and me are boxed in by a pack of Comanches with just one horse and a handful of bullets. Things could damn sure be a sight better, in my estimation."

The Indians talked among themselves, watching the rocks. For a time an eerie silence came to the mountains. Hob noticed the first buzzards circling overhead, drawn by the scent of blood.

The silence grew heavier as Hob watched the Comanches. It was apparent that the Indians couldn't decide what was to be done about the white men. Waiting, Hob felt sweat trickle down his back. When he looked over at Mingus, the cowboy was dozing. His color wasn't right, and blood still seeped from his shoulder.

"A fine fix we're in," Hob muttered, working his palm around the gun butt.

Suddenly, two warriors broke away from the others and trotted their ponies toward Hob. Hob raised his pistol, aiming, when he saw what the two men were after. The wounded Comanche came to his knees. One mounted warrior lifted him off the ground to the back of his pony, then the pair rode away, carrying their injured companion out of range.

"What next?" Hob asked himself as three more Comanches

rode down the slope, staying wide of the rocks. Hob's answer wasn't long in coming . . . the three men began gathering the loose ponies wandering from the battle scene. "Maybe they're pulling out," Hobb said. "Maybe they've had enough."

Hungry buzzards swooped down from the sky, making passes over the dead Indians. One bird landed atop the rump of Hob's dun, squawking, flapping its big wings. "I lost a damn good horse," Hob said, sighing. The dun had carried him countless miles. It was a little bit like losing a good friend.

Mingus groaned, and when Hob looked at his friend he saw the pain in his eyes. Fresh blood covered the front of his shirt. "Help me, Hob," Mingus whispered. "Can't seem to keep my eyes open just now."

Hob hurried over to Mingus, crouching behind rocks to keep from making a target of himself. As he knelt beside Mingus, the cowboy's eyes batted shut and the pistol fell from his hand. He was out cold when Hob lowered him to the ground.

"Lost too much blood," Hob said to himself. "It was that damn fool run to fetch my gun."

He opened Mingus's shirt and tried to stop the blood flow with a piece of bandage. "Damn," Hob muttered, listening to the shallow sounds of each breath Mingus took. "What'll I do?"

With his thumb pressed over the bullet hole, Hob pondered his dilemma. Mingus was too weak to remain conscious. They were down to one horse, and they were still surrounded by Comanches. The other canteen was behind the dun's saddle, along with the rest of the tequila. "Even if those Yamps clear out we're in a fix, ol' hoss," he muttered. "We're two days away from the ranch and down to just one bronc. If the Indians jump us again farther north, we're as good as dead, you and me."

Of course, Mingus couldn't hear him, and he wondered why he was wasting his breath talking to a sleeping man.

A few minutes later, the bleeding stopped. Hob kept an eye over his shoulder as he rewound the bandage. The Comanches were having another parley near the mouth of the pass while the loose ponies were gathered. It was a standoff of sorts; the Indians weren't willing to risk another all-out charge toward the rocks, while Hob and Mingus sure as hell weren't going anyplace, outnumbered as they were.

Hob loosened the cinch on the roan and carried the canteen to Mingus, trying to awaken him just long enough to pour a few swallows of water down his throat, always with an eye toward the Comanches. Beyond the protection of the rocks the buzzards fed on the corpses, a sight too grisly for Hob to watch. When it was clear that the Indians were content to watch the white men without launching another attack, Hob spread Mingus's bedroll beside the boulder and moved him gently to the blankets.

"A waiting game, that's what it is," Hob mumbled, shoving the extra pistol in his belt after checking the loads. "Maybe they'll wait 'til dark before they rush me. They've made it mighty damn plain they don't aim to go someplace else for a while."

He hobbled the roan, just in case, to keep the horse from wandering off. Then he sat down to wait for the Indian's next move. The sun dropped lower below the horizon. Just then, Hob would have given a month's wages for what was left of the tequila in his warbag. With his nerves on edge, he rested behind a rock to watch the Comanches. They sat their ponies, watching him like buzzards perched on a branch.

"They know time is on their side," he said, fingering sweat from his brow. "All they have to do is wait 'til we run out of water, or die of starvation. Damn the lousy luck. As far as I'm concerned, that four-leaf clover don't work at all."

He listened to the sounds of the buzzards feeding on the carcasses, until the sound threatened to drive him mad. Once, he considered wasting a bullet on a bird that flew near the body of the Indian who had come around the back of their hiding place. Hob walked over to the dead warrior, examined the cut of his deerskin leggings and the intricate beadwork decorating his clothing. The Yamparika was typically small and wiry. Had things gone another way, the Yamp would have tortured Hob and Mingus with mindless cruelty, in the Comanche way. Death would have been slow and painful.

When Hob returned to the rocks, he noticed a change in the placement of the warriors. They were spread out around the rock pile, safely out of pistol range.

"They'll wait us out until we're both dead," he said, taking a look at Mingus. "Looks like we'll cash in our chips right here, partner. It's gonna be a hell of a way to die. Never figured it this way. I'd planned to die of old age sittin' in a rocking chair at the Bar B after I got too old to sit a horse. Damn it all, Mr. Strawn, but it looks like our luck has run out."

He thought of Elena Montoya again. Given a chance, he might have gotten to know her and maybe even kisssed her once or twice. Just thinking about it, he felt a tingle in his chest that reminded him of the flutter of a butterfly's wings.

Dark came slowly to the Christmas Mountains. Hob watched the shadows lengthen, fearing another Indian attack when it got too dark to see. At dusk, the vultures flew clumsily into the sky and there was silence. Mingus had not awakened once all afternoon. Hob had never felt so all alone.

A coyote's call echoed from a distant peak. Soon, its mate answered. A desert owl hooted once, as if to announce the coming of night. Stars appeared in the sky, twinkling like tiny lanterns above the mountains. Hob clutched the butt of the pistol with his eyes glued to the battlefield in front of the rocks, dreading the long night ahead of him, wondering if he could stay awake.

Sometime before midnight, Mingus coughed, and the sound made Hob jump. Since nightfall the mountains had been filled with an eerie silence, keeping Hob's nerves on edge. A piece of moon lit up the surrounding slopes, and Hob could see the battlefield clearly. There was no sign of the Comanches, a fact that kept Hob wondering when they would make their next move.

When he heard his partner stir, he crept over to Mingus with the canteen. "Drink some of this," he said, lifting the cowboy's head.

"What happened?" Mingus croaked. "It got dark all of a sudden. What happened to the Indians?"

"You passed out cold, partner . . . lost a lot of blood. No sign of the Comanches."

Mingus took a few swallows of water. "I'll be okay. You keep your eyes peeled. That was some mighty fancy shootin', Mr. Shedd. They'll think twice before they rush us again."

It was an hour past sunup when Hob realized the Comanches were gone. He crept from the rocks, following their hoofprints to the pass. After a careful examination of the rim on either side, he stayed along the tracks until they turned south toward the Mexican border.

"Had a bellyful, I reckon," he said, holstering his Colt.

He trudged back to the rocks, gathering his gear from the dun's carcass before he awakened Mingus. "They pulled out," he told Mingus. "I figure they went looking for easier horses to steal. We didn't have but one left anyways."

He helped Mingus into the saddle and started off on foot, leading the roan. Before they'd gone a couple of miles, Hob's feet hurt. High-heeled cowboy boots didn't make for easy walking, particularly on an uphill climb. He stumbled a time or two. When it was apparent their progress would be too slow, Hob climbed up behind Mingus. The roan was already too long without feed and water; Hob hated himself for what his added weight was doing to the animal, but he saw himself as a man without choices.

CHAPTER 9

IT was well after dark two days later when they rode through the mouth of the horseshoe canyon to the ranch headquarters. It was an end to miles of bitter hardship for the horse and men, existing on meager bits of food and sparse water as they made their way through the Christmas peaks and then across the gentler Santiagos. The roan was gaunt, yet he'd proven his toughness by carrying both men. When they rode past the adobe wall around the main house, the dogs set up a racket. Cowboys spilled from the bunkhouse, carrying lanterns and rifles to see what the ruckus was about. Hob slid painfully from the roan's rump, stiffened by the long ride.

"What happened to Mingus?" Tom Barclay asked, peering at the bloodstain on Mingus's shoulder. "Did you find the boy?"

"It's a long story, Tom." Hob sighed. "Help me carry Mingus to the house so Miz Barclay can see to his wound."

He turned to one of the ranch hands before starting toward the house and said, "Make damn sure this roan gets plenty of grain and water. And rub him down with wet feed sacks. He saved our lives in those mountains."

Tip appeared in the circle of lantern light, questioning Hob with a look. "What about the boy? And the others?" he asked softly.

Hob shook his head, too exhausted to answer properly. "We never got close to 'em. That backshootin' Ranger bushwhacked us in the Chisos."

They sat before the fireplace in hide-bottomed chairs. Hob had eaten like a starved wolf pup, devouring two plates of stew Clara made for him after she finished tending Mingus. They had taken Mingus to a big four-poster bed at the end of the hallway, where Clara had given him swallows of laudanum before attending to his wound.

Hob and Tip and Tom sipped Kentucky whiskey from shot glasses, silent for a time after Hob finished recounting what had happened to Mingus and him. Tom Barclay's face was etched with concern. Hob watched the rancher's eyes.

Tom stared at the fire, deciding what should be done about the missing cowhands. Approaching sixty, he was still as tough as he was the day he came to far west Texas to claim the thousands of acres of land that now bore his name on deed records. He'd wrestled the land from Comanches and Lipans and Mexican bandits and held on to it by the law of the gun for better than thirty years.

Finally, Tom said, "They went off on their own, so what becomes of them is their business. It's the boy I'm worried about. He ain't hardly old enough to understand the consequences of following Soap and Shorty."

"It was a mistake for any of us to head into Mexico on the basis of that letter," Hob admitted. "But at the time we didn't know about that Texas Ranger."

Tom's face clouded. "Tumlinson rode in while you and your crew were out with the branding," he said thoughtfully. "While he watered his horse he asked if we'd seen any strangers. Said he was on the trail of some wanted men. I didn't pay much attention to it at the time . . . not 'til that other feller rode up a few hours behind the Ranger."

Hob stiffened when he heard this piece of news.

"Tom had another visitor," Tip said ominously.

"Gave his name as Brown. By the description Tom gave, I figure I know him."

Hob peered closely at Tip.

"Who do you figure he was?" Hob asked.

Tip's dark eyes flashed with smoldering anger. "If I'm right, he's a bounty hunter by the name of John Frank Brown."

Hob waited for Tip to say more. The muscles in Tip's cheeks worked furiously, and his fingers tightened around the shot glass.

"Who is John Frank Brown?" Hob asked, growing impatient with Tip's silence.

"A killer." Tip sighed, glancing over at Tom. "If it's him, he's after the money and he'll kill anyone and everyone who gets in his way."

Hob pondered this new information as quickly as he could. "Maybe I had things figured wrong," he said, thinking back to the ambush. "Could have been Brown who bushwhacked us. We did find another set of tracks in those mountains."

Tom poured more whiskey into his glass from the bottle near his feet. "When Tip told me about your hunch that the Ranger had turned bad, I had my doubts," he said. "I consider myself a pretty good judge of men, and I didn't have Tumlinson pegged for a thief. I didn't pay much attention to him at the time, but he didn't seem the sort who'd sell his badge. He don't have the appearance of a coward who'll shoot a feller from the dark."

"What did Brown say he wanted?" Hob asked his boss.

Tom shrugged. "Same as the Ranger. Asked if I'd seen any strangers recently headed toward Mexico. I told him about Tumlinson. He didn't act surprised . . . like he already knew."

"It makes sense," Hob said, staring vacantly at the floor, "that a bounty hunter would be after that much loot. But Shorty and Soap will have Scoop in the line of fire if they lead John Frank Brown to the right cave. Wonder if Tumlinson knows that Brown is down there too?"

Tom Barclay had no answer.

"Hard to say," Tip observed. "It'll be like a game of cat-and-mouse. Tumlinson is tracking our friends and Brown is tracking Tumlinson. One thing's for sure: if our men find that money, they'll never get out of that canyon alive if that bounty hunter turns out to be John Frank Brown. And unless Carl Tumlinson is one hell of a hand with a gun, he'll wind up dead same as the others."

"We've got to do something," Hob whispered. "We can't just sit here and wait for the bad news. If you're not opposed to it, Mr. Barclay, I'll gather some clean clothes and a sackful of grub and saddle a fresh horse."

Tom gave Hob a warning look. "You're not a gunfighter, Hob," he said. "You're liable to get yourself killed down there."

Hob tossed down his whiskey. "Those are my men. Reckon it's fair to say they're my friends, to boot. The kid don't deserve to die like that, and I figure Soap and Shorty could use a hand if that bounty hunter jumps 'em."

Just then Tom shook his head, as if his mind was made up against Hob's idea.

"Hold off until morning, Hob," he said. "I'll sleep on it. There are other things; we've got a ranch to run, cattle that need tending to. Pine Springs is just about dry, and Pinion Springs is mighty low, according to Sancho. It's been a dry summer, and we may have to drive those high-country herds to the river 'til it rains. You're foreman on this ranch. If I let you ride off to those Mexican mountains, you could be down there until the snow flies. We've got to think of the cattle first, and we're four hands short right now, what with three down in Mexico and Mingus laid up for a spell. If it wasn't for Scoop bein' down there . . ."

Tom didn't finish his remark. He didn't have to. Hob understood the rancher's dilemma. The herds had to come first, as always.

"The boy is sixteen," Tip said. "He ain't some wet-nosed baby anymore. A boy has to grow up sometime and face the music when he makes a bad choice."

Hob stood up, stretching stiff muscles.

"If you're right about John Frank Brown," Hob replied,

"Scoop may not get the chance to learn from his first mistake. It's my fault, for lettin' him go in the first place."

Hob stalked out of the house. He entered the bunkhouse and met silent stares from the men seated on the bunks. Expectant faces awaited word about the three missing cowhands. "Tell us what happened, Hob," someone said from a dark corner.

Hob sat on his bunk, pulled off his boots, and told the men what had happened. ". . . Mingus got shot by a bushwhacker, and I had no choice but to bring him back to the ranch. Whilst we were in the Christmases, we were hit by a band of Comanches and we lost one horse. Mingus is hurt bad, but I reckon he'll make it now. For three days I've been cussing a Texas Ranger, figuring he was the one who shot Mingus. I didn't know about the bounty hunter until just now."

"John Frank Brown," Chick said, seated on the bunk across from Hob. "According to Tip, Brown is one hell of a gunhand."

Hob shook his head sadly. "Scoop's caught in the middle, riding with Shorty and Soap. That's about the emptiest country I ever rode through. It would be easy for Brown to ambush 'em, just like he did me and Mingus."

Sancho Alvarez pointed a finger south. "There are many *banditos* in those mountains also. If they see the tracks of only a few horses, they will follow them and try to rob the men . . . maybe so to steal their horses. Those Chisos . . . they are a bad place, *compadre*. There are some who say the most famous bandito in all of Mexico has his hideout in the Chisos near Ojinaga. If Luis Zambrano finds our three *compadres,* he will surely kill them for their horses and saddles."

Hob tossed his hat to the foot of his bunk before he rested his head on his pillow. "Those Yamparikas who jumped us headed south toward the border. When a man starts to add up the troubles down there, he can run out of fingers to count 'em on. I asked the boss man to let me ride back to lend the boys a hand. Tom said he'd let me know in the morning, but there's work to be done around here and we're shorthanded, so there's a chance Tom won't let me go."

An uneasy silence gripped the men. Everyone was thinking about the dangers the three Bar B riders faced south of the river. Tip entered the bunkhouse some time later, casting an eye toward Hob as he walked to his bunk and hung his gunbelt from a peg.

"Tom's worried," Tip said. "He's torn betwixt an' between. He knows Miz Barclay loves Scoop, almost like he was her own. Tom don't say so, but I reckon he feels about the same. Still, the ranch comes first, and he ain't paying our wages for us to ride all over Mexico when some fool kid gets himself in trouble."

The next morning Tom Barclay's face was gray when he met Hob in front of the cookshack. "Mornin', Hob," he said. "Didn't sleep much last night, worryin' about what should be done. Clara, she says every last one of us oughta ride down there to fetch the men out of Mexico. That's a woman for you . . . never looking at the other side of things." Tom shoved his hands in his pockets, watching the sunrise.

"I'll go, Mr. Barclay, if that's what you want."

Tom chewed his lip thoughtfully. "I'm not sure what to do just now. If I send anyone, it won't be you, because I need you here. Besides, you're no match for a gunslinger, Hob. I'd have it on my conscience if that bounty hunter put a bullet in you. No, I suppose it oughta be Tip, since he's handy with a six-gun. What's your idea on it, Hob?"

It wasn't like Tom to ask Hob for his opinion.

"I figure you should ask Tip if the notion suits him," Hob replied. "He hired on with this outfit to work cattle."

Tom sighed, as though the matter weighed heavily on his mind.

"You're right," he said. "First off, I've got to decide if it's worth the risk."

Tom started for the house, visibly weighed down by the burden of having to make a decision about this. Hob watched him climb the porch steps, then looked at the little grove of trees near the back of the canyon where Tom and Clara's only child lay beneath a weathered grave marker. The child died at birth, and, according to Tom, Clara could not have any more children . . . something had gone wrong inside her. That was the reason Clara had taken to Scoop so quickly when the orphan boy came to the ranch. He needed mothering, and Clara needed someone to mother. Her attachment to the boy would make Tom's decision much tougher, and there was hardly a one of the hands who didn't see the kid as a member of the family.

Later that morning, right after Hob paid a visit on Mingus at the house, the issue over the ride to Mexico was settled by another turn of events. Tinker Barnes had galloped in from the line shack at Pine Springs to say the pool had gone bone dry the day before. Hob listened to the news, checking his tally book. By his rough count, over four hundred head of longhorns depended upon the spring. Those cattle would have to be driven south to the river, since the pool at Pinion Springs was already too low to support more cattle until it rained. If it ever rained again, Hob thought. There was no time to waste.

"I'll tell the boss," Hob said. "Get everybody mounted on fresh horses. It's gonna take every hand on the place to drive so many thirsty cattle. Tell Cookie to fix us enough grub for a week."

Hob knew that thirsty cattle instinctively would scatter all over the Santiagos, searching for pockets of rainwater in the dry mountain streambeds. It was going to be one hell of a job, rounding up so many wandering longhorns. Most of the older cows were as wild as deer. Efforts to drive them in any direction would be hard on horses and men.

As he hurried toward the house to give Tom the news, his mind wandered to Scoop and the two older cowboys down in the empty canyons of Chihuahua. Whatever dangers they faced would have to be met without help from the Bar B.

CHAPTER 10

HOB rested his gray gelding on the side of a mountain with an eye on Chick and Jim Bob riding a dry wash below, pushing a handful of mossy-horned cows in front of them. For three days they'd ridden the high country above Pine Springs, gathering the strays the rest of the men missed when they drove the main bunch south. Tip and Cookie worked to hold the big herd in a southerly direction. (Cookie joined the roundup since Scoop was Tip's regular partner and two men were needed, working in pairs.) Sancho and his cousin Lupe cleared the brushy flats west of the dry spring while Tinker and Billy Klegg swept the northernmost stretches. It fell to Hob to guide the strays toward the main herd, a job that required moving to the highest ground to direct the men with their cattle. Most of the time, Hob saw nothing but dust in the distance where Tip and Cookie held the herd.

"Can't be many more," Hob said to himself. "Time we headed for the river."

He raised his pistol and fired two shots, a signal they'd agreed upon at breakfast that would end the search for more strays. The shots echoed through the silent Santiagos, then Hob reined the gray toward the cloud of dust in the distance.

I hope the kid is okay, Hob thought. *Soap and Shorty, too, even though they don't deserve it. Damn them to hell and back for talking Scoop into staying with them.*

For three days they rode the high lonesome above the dry spring. Now and then Hob would think about Mingus, worrying about his friend's shoulder, deciding that Mingus was probably propped up in bed on a pile of feather pillows eating Clara's fancy cooking. *She's likely baked him a cake by now,* Hob reasoned, certain that his partner could wheedle something special out of Clara if he complained loudly enough. *If he's been eatin' fancy sugar cakes whilst I'm out here sleepin' on this hard ground, I'm liable to put a bullet in his good shoulder when I get back,* Hob thought. He would never have admitted it to anyone else, but he found himself missing Mingus on the cattle drive. "Even those long-winded stories would sound good right about now," Hob muttered, spurring the gray down the mountain.

He rode to the herd and found Tip. Tip was layered with caliche and sweat, trying to keep the longhorns moving into a southerly breeze. "Can't hold 'em without some help," Tip complained, pointing to three more maverick steers trotting away from the herd, bawling for water.

"Help's coming," Hob replied, turning in his saddle to look for the last bunches of strays being driven toward the herd. "I signaled everybody to come in. Let's head 'em south, Mr. Giles."

They spread out to push the rear of the herd. Cookie galloped his lathered sorrel through the dust cloud until he was alongside Hob. "Move 'em out!" Hob shouted.

In short order, Sancho and Lupe joined the herd with a handful of strays. Then Chick and Jim Bob trotted off a rise behind a dozen loose-hided longhorns and whitefaced calves. An hour later, Tinker and Billy caught up driving a single brindled cow, a true mossy-horn with a six-foot spread bearing a Rafter Bar brand. She was a neighbor's cow, if you could call a ranch two days to the north a neighbor. Ike Ault owned the Rafter Bar, and his brindled stray had taken up with the Bar B herd at Pine Springs. When the two ranches joined forces for the drive to the railhead, the Rafter Bar cow would be returned. Hob wondered how many cows they'd missed in the mountains. Whatever the number, they would be left to fend for themselves.

It was a peaceful picture. The longhorns were spread out along the riverbank at dusk the following day, some belly-deep in the river, drinking their fill. Nine trail-weary cowboys sat their horses on a rise above the river to watch the end of the dusty cattle drive.

"Done," Hob said, knocking dust from his shirt with a swipe of his hat brim. "We can make the bunkhouse before midnight. Let's ride."

They swung west, then north toward the horseshoe canyon outlined against the night sky. Conversation was rare on the ride home. Cookie complained about his saddle sores, unaccustomed as he was to anything besides a wagon seat. The others were thinking about their bunks, too tired to care when Cookie voiced his objections to a faster pace.

Hob was last to strip his saddle from his horse, alone in the moonlight when he heard footsteps coming toward him from the house. He recognized Tom and waved a greeting before he hung his saddle in the shed.

He knew something was wrong when he saw Tom's face in the lantern light as the rancher came into the saddle shed. He'd learned to read the boss man's expressions like some men could read a book.

"How'd it go?" Tom asked, peering under Hob's hat brim.

"We made it to the river with all but a few," Hob replied. "Couldn't hold the main bunch together any longer, so we drove what we had to water. We counted three hundred and ninety-six mother cows. It's damn sure dry up in those mountains, boss. I don't remember it ever being so dry before."

Tom shook his head, fidgeting, as though he had more to say. "Tully rode in from Pinion Springs yesterday." He sighed. "It's down to mud. The cattle are gettin' bogged when they come to drink. Tully picked up a string of fresh horses and two more ropes. He said he and Carl are wearin' out horses and ropes pulling bogged cattle out of the spring.

I know you and the boys are worn down to a frazzle, Hob, but Tully says we've got two or three more days before Pinion Springs goes dry. Got no choice but to bring those cattle down from the mountains too."

Hob let his shoulders drop. He and the men had spent eighteen hours in the saddle today. They were too exhausted to ride until they'd had a few hours of sleep.

"We'll snooze for a couple of hours," Hob said, "then we'll head for Pinion Springs."

Tom nodded, forcing a grin. "Mingus is better," he said, knowing Hob would ask. "Clara baked him a plum pie. Come to the house before you leave: Mingus has been askin' about you every day . . . if we've had any word."

"Plum pie," Hob said wistfully, his mouth watering. For most of a week, he and the hands had existed on dry jerky and coffee. "I feel really sorry for Mingus, laid up like he is, havin' to choke down a whole plum pie all by himself."

Tom chuckled. "There's enough for everybody. Clara baked a whole batch with the last of the plums. You and the men stop by the house before you ride out." Tom started for the door, then hesitated. "I reckon you know I'd lend a hand if I could. I can't leave Clara and Mingus with the place to themselves. Somebody has to draw water from the wells for the saddle stock and the bulls. Ride careful, Hob, and stop by the house on your way to the spring."

Hob shook his head and started for the bunkhouse, trudging along on bone-weary feet. Pinion Springs was a day and a half north of the ranch. During the summer, Carl Wade and A. J. Tully tended to the cattle from the line shack beside the spring, a lonely outpost high in the Santiagos near Black Horse Peak. He knew the two cowboys would have their hands full, pulling thirsty cattle from the mud, now that the spring pool was running dry. When the men in the bunkhouse heard the news, there would be bellyaching aplenty. Hob couldn't blame them much, but it was a cowboy's lot to work from sunup 'til dark anyway—the hours got longer during a drought and at branding time. This year, the two events had come together, doubling the load on the men.

Hob lay across his bunk and was asleep in seconds. He hadn't bothered to pull off his boots or his gun.

They sat their horses in front of the big adobe house, eating slices of sweet plum pie. The house always reminded Hob of a fortress, which it had been in earlier years when Indians and bandits roamed freely across Barclay range. Hob savored the delicious pie slowly, until Mingus hobbled out on the porch wearing a grin, dressed in one of Tom's long white nightshirts.

"If you ain't a sight," Hob said, chuckling. "I thought I was seein' a ghost, dark as it is just now and you dressed up in a white bedsheet. How's the shoulder?"

"Near good as new," Mingus replied. "I argued that I was well enough to go along to Pinion Springs, but the boss lady said no, so I'll have to suffer a while longer in that big bed."

Some of the men hooted, in a better mood after the plum pie.

"We can see you're suffering somethin' awful," Hob said. "Be careful whilst we're gone, ol' hoss. I'd hate to hear that you took a terrible fall off that mattress while we're at Pinion Springs."

Cookie guffawed at the idea. "Don't break any bones, Mr. Strawn, and don't get yourself foundered on all Miz Barclay's good cookin' while I'm gone. Soon as I get back I'll fix you some regular stew, so you won't get sorefooted eatin' all that rich food."

The men laughed, then Hob reined his horse toward the gate in the adobe wall. "Be seein' you, partner," he said. "Get well quick as you can so you can tell me more of those windy stories. It was so damn quiet this past week that I asked Cookie to bang a spoon against the coffeepot last night, just to see if maybe I'd gone stone deaf."

Mingus grinned and waved as Hob spurred for the gate.

Not a word had been said about Scoop or the other two cowboys. Hob knew the missing men weighed heavily on everyone's mind, but there was work to be done. Hundreds of Bar B cattle would die unless they were taken to water, a job that would require every cowboy on the ranch. Trotting across the moonlit yard, Hob knew it was breaking Clara Barclay's heart that no one had gone looking for Scoop. Perhaps keeping busy nursing Mingus had helped keep her mind off worrying about the kid.

A mile north of the canyon, crossing dry caliche flats that stretched to the foothills of the Santiagos, Cookie let loose with a string of cusswords. "Goddamn any outfit that'd ask a man to ride such a contraption as this," he shouted, standing in his stirrups to ease the pain of his saddle sores. "The first feller to invent a saddle with a pillow tied to the seat will make himself a rich man. This goddamn sorry excuse for a saddle I'm ridin' ain't worth a pinch of snuff. I'd sooner sit in a clump of prickly pear as to ride a Tom Barclay saddle. I hired on with this outfit to cook grub and drive a chuck wagon, damn it! My butt's so sore it feels like I'm sittin' on needles."

Some of the men laughed. Tinker Barnes rode up beside Cookie and tipped his hat, showing off his bald spot in the light from the stars. "Ridin' a saddle for thirty-two years is what made all my hair fall out," Tinker said. "Watch yourself, Cookie, or you'll lose all them chin whiskers, seein' as you're already bald on top. There's somethin' about saddle leather that makes hair so it won't grow."

"I reckon that makes you safe from Injuns," Cookie growled, still testy in spite of the laughter around him. "No sense in scalping a man who ain't got one."

Hob grinned, now that the men seemed to be in better spirits. It was a cowboy's way to joke about his lot, especially after so many weary hours spent on a horse. Earlier, when Hob had rolled the men out and told them about the spring, there had been some grumbling. They faced another few days in their saddles and nights on hard ground, gathering the Pinion Springs herd. All things considered, the complaining wasn't as bad as it might have been. There wasn't a cowboy among them who didn't know what a drought did to thirsty cattle. Bleached bones could be found all over the ranch where cattle died during a dry year.

Hob was distracted from his ruminations when Cookie started cussing again, as they rode up the first rocky slope into the Santiagos. "A man's ass just ain't built to sit a damn saddle," Cookie shouted, his face twisted as though he suffered terrible pain. "If this goddamn bay horse don't find himself a gentler gait, I aim to shoot the son of a bitch right betwixt his ears. I'll walk the rest of the way, after I set fire to this damn miserable saddle."

At noon they halted long enough to eat the sackful of biscuits Clara Barclay had made, washing them down with swallows from their canteens. Hob was constantly watching the horizon, on the lookout for more Comanches. It was late in the year for Indians to be on the prowl so far south of their usual range, especially Yamparikas. Yamps occupied the middle of the Comanche Nation, the upper Concho River and lands to the east, neighbors to the Noconas he'd known as a boy. The Kwahadics roamed the Staked Plains north and west, holding tribal lands from the encroachment of Apaches. Something big was afoot to bring Yamps to the Rio Grande country, a thought that kept Hob on edge as they rode higher into the Santiago Mountains.

The land was dry as they continued north. They found widely scattered herds of Bar B longhorns grazing the slopes and high-country meadows. Hob noticed the flanks of the cows: the younger animals were drawn, bearing the hollow look any seasoned cowboy recognized when cattle were having difficulty finding water. The older longhorns were smarter, grazing lower pastures where tiny pockets of spring rainwater still lay hidden in shallow pools beneath piles of rock in dry streambeds, away from the evaporation of summer suns. All the while, as they climbed the Santiagos, Hob swept the ground for sign of unshod ponies.

Dark put them in silent peaks and empty valleys. A few deer bounded away from the approaching horses as they rode to a dry ravine to make a night camp.

Hob sent Tinker and Sancho to ride out the dry streambed to look for pocket water while Cookie built a fire and boiled coffee. The rest of the men lay on the ground, resting their backsides, allowing their horses to graze on the meager grass in the ravine.

"Driest year I ever saw," Hob said when Tip stretched out on his bedroll beside the fire. "I figure that's what has those Comanches on the move. The buffalo herds have moved north to find better grazing. Yamps can't find any buffalo, so they're hunting deer."

"Just so they aren't hunting scalps," Tip replied. "Why do you think they jumped you and Mingus?"

"Only two of us. Had us figured for easy pickings."

Soon the smell of coffee started Hob's belly grumbling. A cool night breeze came from the southwest. Stars twinkled overhead. Before Hob realized it, he dozed off.

Tinker and Sancho returned, awakening Hob with the sounds of their horses. "Found a place to water our broncs," Tinker said, stepping gingerly from his saddle, then working the stiffness from his knees. "We rolled the rocks away. It's less than a mile. Never remember so much trouble findin' water before, Hob. We'll lose a bunch of cattle before this dry spell is over."

Hob rubbed sleep from his eyes as he came to the fire.

"It's damn sure dry," he said, pouring himself a cup of steaming coffee. "Tom's worried. I can see it on his face."

"That ain't all he's worried about, Mr. Shedd," Cookie remarked, passing strips of jerky to the men. "It's the kid and Shorty and Soap that's botherin' him. If it wasn't for this dry spell and those played-out springs, some of you'd be on your way to Mexico to look for 'em."

"Any fool can see it's eatin' on him," Hob agreed. "It's my fault, lettin' them go in the first place."

"It was the whiskey," Cookie said. "Shorty got to talking about how he was gonna be a rich man when he found that loot, and the kid believed him. They were ridin' in and out of them big canyons, dreamin' about all the things they were gonna buy with that money. Hell, Hob, before me and Mingus pulled out for Ojinaga, the three of them already had half that money spent."

Hob shook his head. "Well, they're on their own. I just hope they've got enough sense to keep their eyes open for that bounty hunter. Maybe Shorty and Soap have run out of whiskey by now."

Tip grunted. "It won't matter. Drunk or sober, they won't be a match for John Frank Brown. The best we can hope for is that they can't find the money."

Billy Klegg caught Hob's attention when he spoke. "I saw that Brown feller when he rode past Pine Springs. Rode down to water his horse. I asked him if he was lost. He didn't give me an answer . . . just thanked me for the water and rode on. I could tell by the way he was ridin' that he was following a set of tracks. Kept his eyes to the ground, movin' real slow."

"Following that feller Cobb, most likely," Hob said. "I figure he's the one who hung Dave Cobb, although it still could've been the Ranger. Either way, both of them are down in Chihuahua right now, and one of them is a bushwhacker."

Billy tossed down the rest of his coffee. "The gent who showed up at Pine Springs could damn sure be a bush-whacker. If I'm any judge of character, that feller had a mighty ugly disposition and he knew his way around a gun. Wore a side-pull holster across his belly. . . . A quick-draw artist, plain as day."

Tip shook his head, staring at the fire. "That'll be John Frank," he said softly.

"There's nothing we can do about it now," Hob declared,

climbing tiredly to his feet. "We've got cattle to move from these mountains. Tighten your cinches, boys. We're wasting time."

Cookie doused the fire and tied the coffeepot on the packhorse while the men cinched their saddles for the ride. When the men were mounted, they followed Tinker and Sancho down the dry wash to the collected rainwater, where the horses drank their fill.

Hob struck an easy trot at the front of the procession as they rode out of the draw toward higher ground. In the dark the Santiagos loomed large in front of them. In the days to come, Hob knew he and his men would scour every nook and cranny of those peaks, looking for strays. It held the promise of a hard week in the saddle.

They rode down into the Pinion Springs basin an hour past dawn. Hob saw the mud around the drying spring pool and the deep cattle tracks where watering animals had bogged down. To the east sat the line riders' one-room cabin and a pole corral. Hob remembered the cabin and the howling winter storm when he and Mingus were trapped inside by the snow. If any place on earth could be described as lonesome, it was the Pinion Springs line shack in winter.

A plume of smoke curled from the chimney. Hob saw the door crack open when the sounds of their horses filled the basin. Tully stuck his head out, dressed in red long-handled underwear and boots, saluting the Bar B cowboys with his tin coffee cup as the men rode up to the shack.

"Glad you made it when you did," Tully said, grinning and jerking a thumb toward the spring. "Me an' Carl are plumb wore out, dragging cows from that mud."

Hob eyed the pool at the center of the basin. Less than a foot of water remained. "The boss said to gather everything we can find and drive 'em to the river. Cookie'll fix us a bite of breakfast and then we'll start combing the mountains."

Carl came out on the little front porch just then. His jeans and shirt were covered with dried mud. Even his face bore a smear across one cheek. "We've been up to our eyelashes in mud around here," he said. "Damn glad to see you, Hob. Some of the older cows and the calves are too weak to pull themselves out when they come in to water. Me an' Tully have stretched every rope we've got til they're half a mile long and thin as fiddle strings. Another day and we'd have a bunch of dead cattle on our hands."

Hob stepped to the ground, testing his legs, trying to rub some feeling back into them.

CHAPTER 11

THEY set out in pairs to bring the cattle from the northern Santiagos to a winding valley below the spring. Hob left Cookie at the line shack to prepare an evening meal over the potbellied stove while he and Tip searched for cows. Before they'd ridden a mile up the switchbacks, they encountered thirsty cattle on their way to water. It fell to Chick and Jim Bob to pull the cows out of the mud, dallying ropes to their saddle horns if one of the weaker animals got bogged down. Sancho and Lupe were given the chore of building a wooden trough and rigging buckets and ropes so water could be hoisted from the shrinking pool and then carried to the watering trough away from the dangerous sucking mud. Planks from the shed were to be laid across the mud for the bucket crew, to keep the men from sinking. It was a temporary solution, until the cows were down from the mountains, or until the spring went completely dry.

To the west, he could see Tully and Carl riding a barren ridge. For the next few days the men would be bunching wild longhorns in some of the roughest country on the Barclay ranch. Finding all the wide-ranging cattle in this section was always a chore. Now the job was made tougher by the scarcity of water. The older cows would go off by themselves, sniffing out hidden seeps and potholes in the rocks.

Hob and Tip rode into a high meadow dotted with pinion and scrub pine. Sun-dried grass grew thick beneath the trees. A squirrel chattered a warning when the horses appeared in the quiet meadow. A cloudless blue sky hung over the mountains, without any promise of rain. On the far side of the clearing a multicolored longhorn cow threw up her tail, snorting when she saw the pair of horsemen. She trotted through a patch of shade beneath a pine tree, disappearing in the shadows with her whitefaced calf.

"Time to go to work," Hob said, shaking out his lariat to build a loop. He spurred the grulla gelding after the cow, scattering a covey of quail as he galloped through the knee-high grass.

Three more cows joined the first, making a dash for higher ground. Hob yelled and slapped his rope against one leg of his leather chaps, trying to spook the longhorns away from the slope so Tip could start them down the mountain.

They worked their way north through the morning hours, driving the cows in twos and threes to the trail they followed into the peaks. Herded together, the longhorns would remain bunched for a few hours more until the men returned to drive them toward the spring. There were always a few mavericks straying off, cows that wouldn't allow themselves to be driven by a horse and rider. Those required a rope around the base of their horns so they could be dragged to the right spot, bellowing and fighting the pull of the rope every step of the way. The work was hard on horses, made worse by the rocky ground. Before noon, Hob's grulla was lathered, puffing for wind.

Later, as Hob followed cattle tracks up a rocky draw between giant slabs of stone, he rounded a turn and rode up on an unusual sight. At the back of the draw, four mossy-horned cows grazed peacefully beside an old buffalo bull. The bull was lame in a foreleg, hopping clumsily from one bunch of grass to the next on three legs. When the buffalo sighted the horse and rider he whirled to face Hob, lowering his head, bellowing once as if he would charge.

"Take it easy, grandpa," Hob said chuckling, slowing his horse. The buffalo was so old his shaggy coat had turned gray around the muzzle. Hob could see the injury to his leg was long since healed. He guessed the crippled bull had been left behind years before when he couldn't stay up with the herd, and now he foraged in the mountains on his own. "I haven't got the heart to put a bullet in you, gramps," he said, reining past the spot where the bull stood his ground. "Hope you don't get too lonesome up here all by yourself, but I've got to take these cows along with me."

Hob drove the longhorns back down the draw, avoiding the old bull's territory as much as he could when he rode past. Somehow the buffalo had made it on just three good legs without being detected during the fall roundups. Hob decided the bull's elusiveness was proof of just how wild and empty these mountains could be.

Hob's grulla had begun to limp. They had chased wild cattle over some mighty rough ground since morning, and it didn't surprise Hob that the mouse-colored horse had come up with a stone bruise.

"Let's start back down with what we've got," he said when Tip rode up beside him. The sun was still three hours above the horizon as they started down the mountains, and Hob wondered how the work was going at the spring. Hob counted thirty-four head of grown cows as the tally for their day's labor. If the other pairs of cowboys had done as well, there was a chance that the Pinion Springs drive would be done before the week was out.

Tip sleeved sweat from his forehead. "Ain't no rougher country in God's creation," he said, "but it's a mighty pretty spot up here. A cowhand's life ain't so awful bad."

Hob scanned the silent peaks, remembering the flatland farms along the Brazos he'd known as a boy. "Pretty don't seem the right word, not for a place where it's so damn dry. Hard to say why I like it up here. Maybe it's the peace and quiet. You're right about one thing, Tip: a cowboy's life beats most anything else when it comes to ways of making a living. The work's hard an' Lord knows the hours are long, but I don't reckon I'd trade this job for a plow handle."

Tip's face hardened. "Same could be said for using a gun.

A cowboy can lay down to sleep without keeping one eye open. The same can't be said for some professions."

Tip seldom mentioned his past as a shootist. At one time or another, every cowhand on the place wondered about it. Tip never discussed the subject, so Hob assumed it was something he wanted to forget. "Out here, a man gets himself measured by what he can do with a rope and a branding iron," Hob said, watching the cows meander down the slopes in front of their horses. "I came west when the war was over. I'd had a bellyful of killing and dying. Carpetbaggers took our farm whilst I was off fightin' with Hood. No reason to stay around Waco, so I saddled my bronc and rode west 'til I found the emptiest place I'd ever been. This is it." Hob grinned, sweeping a hand around the Santiagos.

Tip shook his head in understanding. "I suppose I done the same. A few years back, I took stock of my life and I didn't like what I saw. I was headed down a dead-end trail." He looked across at Hob. "You ever kill a man in a gunfight?" he asked.

Hob thought about the men who died in front of his gun in Virginia and Tennessee. "I killed a fair share in the war. I used to see 'em in my sleep. Some wasn't much more than kids."

Tip worked the muscles in his jaw. "It ain't an easy thing to forget . . . not if a man has a conscience. I'm done with guns, Hob. I don't aim to shoot another feller again, unless I've got no other selection."

Hob thought of Tom Barclay's idea to send Tip to look for Scoop and realized it would be wrong to ask Tip to tangle with the bounty hunter.

"Well," Hob said firmly. "the boss man hired us to swing a loop. I reckon that's all he expects."

Tip eyed Hob just then, and the look was full of concern. "If the boy ain't back when we get these cattle to the river, Tom will send somebody down to look for him. I'll go, Hob. It just so happens that I've made the acquaintance of John

Frank Brown. I'll go after the boy. Just thought I'd make mention of it. The boy was my partner."

Hob was surprised by Tip's offer. "I'll pass the word along," he promised.

They skirted the cows and hurried them down a twisting ravine as the sun moved lower. Hob tried not to think about the missing cowboys or the bounty hunter, forcing his attention to the wild cattle until they neared the spring.

Hob inspected the wooden trough when they entered the basin. Sancho and Lupe gave the joints a coat of roof tar, making the trough watertight. A line of planks ran across the mud to the pool, resting on corral posts. As the cows and calves came to water, the men carried buckets from the spring to refill the trough.

"How many have been driven down so far?" Hob asked when Chick sauntered over from the cabin.

"Tully and Carl got better than fifty. No sign of the rest just yet."

Hob watched Jim Bob drive the cattle out of the basin to bunch them with the others. It was a good first day's gather. If the other riders had similar luck, the mountains could be cleared of the seven hundred mother cows in a week. Hob judged the depth of the pool. The water would run out before the herd was gathered.

"The spring won't last," Hob began, casting a glance over his shoulder at the mountains. "Come sunup I want every man in his saddle early. Two men can hold the main bunch in the valley while the rest of us look for strays. Cookie can carry water to the trough. We're running out of time."

Their faces were covered with bandanas to keep out the choking cloud of dust. A southerly breeze lifted the swirling caliche and swept it over the men riding drag behind the herd, covering them with yellow dust. The dust cloud worsened when the cattle scented water; thirsty cries came from the cows at the front of the bunch as they broke into a trot toward the river. Hob signaled the men at the rear and led them wide of the boiling dust. When they reached higher ground, the men halted to watch the sight as the first cows spilled over the riverbank to drink their fill.

"That's damn sure a big bunch of cattle," Billy announced, standing in his stirrups to view the far side of the herd.

"Not as big as it should have been." Hob sighed, pulling the bandana from his face. They were almost a hundred head short by the tally book. The spring had gone dry two days before, and there was no choice but to head for the river with the animals they had.

"Couldn't be helped," Tinker declared. "We'd have lost the rest of 'em if we'd waited any longer."

Hearing the truth of things didn't make the news any easier to bear. Hob knew some of the cattle they left behind would survive on pocket water. When the herds were driven to high grazing in the spring, they would find the bones of the ones that didn't make it. Only then would the drought's toll be counted.

"I've got an announcement to make, boys," Cookie said, leaning forward in his saddle at an odd angle so his weight was off the seat of his pants. "I'm swearin' an oath never to sit a saddle until my Maker calls me to my grave. Should Tom Barclay ever tell me to mount a horse again, I swear I'll quit this damn outfit and walk all the way to El Paso before I'll do it. And come tomorrow, if the stew seems a little on the tough side, you can bet your boots it'll be this rough-gaited bay you're eatin'. I'm gonna kill him, boys, and put the meat in the stew. He damn sure ain't fit to ride."

First Tinker, then Billy, started to laugh. The others pulled dust-caked bandanas from their faces to laugh along with the rest. Hob laughed, too, in spite of the ache in his joints and the dust in this throat. Hob supposed the laughter was mostly relief that the drive was over. They'd been eight days gathering the Pinion Springs cattle, then driving them to the river. Hob couldn't ever remember being so tired.

"Let's head home," he said, reining toward the horseshoe canyon in the distance.

They held their foot-sore broncs to a walk under a noon-day sun, feeling the heat rise from the ocotillo flats as they rode toward the ranch. Now and then Hob looked at the sky, wondering if it would ever rain again on Bar B land. For days he'd been too tired to think about rain, or much of anything else. He and the men had their hands full holding so many thirsty cattle together. Now, as they neared the ranch head-quarters, he found himself thinking about Scoop and the missing cowboys. *I wonder if Tom's had any word,* he thought, sighting the mouth of the canyon and the adobe wall around the house.

They rode slowly past the house toward the barns and corrals as the dogs barked a greeting. Hob stopped at the gate and swung down, handing Tinker his reins so the horse could be put away and fed properly. Hob started toward the porch, knocking dust from himself with his hat, looking forward to seeing his old partner. "Hope the shoulder is better," he said aloud as his spurs clanked over the packed caliche.

Tom came out on the porch just as Hob noticed a buggy that was parked with empty shafts in the shade of a live oak tree. Hob was about to ask about the buggy when he saw another figure come out of the house behind Tom. Hob recognized the visitor, and his feet simply stopped moving.

"Glad to see you, Hob," Tom said. "I saw the dust near the river. How did it go?"

Hob's tongue wouldn't work quite right when he tried to give Tom an answer, distracted as he was by the woman.

"We have guests, Hob," Tom said. "I understand you in-vited the Montoyas to the Bar B. We've been showing them around until you got back."

Hob felt suddenly dizzy. Remembering his manners, he pulled off his hat. "Seems every time we've met I'm in need of a bath," he said, deciding the fates were against him when it came to Elena Montoya. "Good to see you again."

The woman smiled, and Hob was sure his knees would buckle before he made it to the porch rail.

CHAPTER 12

HOB settled on a bench after the introductions and hand-shakes, conscious of the woman's glances as she helped Clara pour whiskey for the men. Don Miguel seemed more at ease in Hob's presence, listening to Hob describe the cattle drive. They sat in the shade of the ramada east of the house, sipping whiskey, enjoying the cool breeze. Tom appeared to be satisfied with the cattle count.

"Under the circumstances, I'd say you did the best you could, Hob. Some of the cows you missed will survive."

Don Miguel watched Hob with interest. "You and your vaqueros must be very tired," he said. "Senor Barclay is a very lucky man to have hardworking men in his employ."

Hob accepted the compliment in silence, worrying about his appearance. Now and then he stole looks at Elena, half expecting to find her nose wrinkling when his smell reached her. His clothes were caked with sweat and yellow dust, and his face sported two weeks of unshaven stubble. He had carefully selected a bench downwind.

"I'm sure the men are exhausted," Tom began. "I'll tell them how much I appreciate the extra work."

Hob shook his head, toying with his glass. It was an effort to keep his eyes from straying to Elena Montoya. Somehow, he'd forgotten just how beautiful she was. Long black hair framed her smooth oval face. Her eyes reminded Hob of a whitetail doe. She wore denims and a soft white blouse. When Hob felt her eyes on him he squirmed, and when she smiled at him a tiny tremor entered his fingers.

He became aware of a difference in Clara, a vague uneasi-ness as she sat beside Elena, not taking part in the conversation. Hob wondered if the change in Clara had anything to do with Mingus and the healing of his wound.

"How's my partner?" Hob asked, directing his question to Clara. "Has he been driving you crazy while we were gone?"

The color quickly left Clara's face. "He's with you, isn't he?"

Hob stiffened, coming erect on the edge of the bench. "No. Why would he be with us?"

"Oh, Tom," Clara cried, clasping her hands before her face. "I knew something was wrong. Mingus didn't ride out to meet the herd!"

Tom Barclay's expression turned grave. "He rode off yesterday morning. Said he was feeling better. I couldn't talk him out of going. He said he felt terrible about leaving you shorthanded. His wound was healed over, so I gave up arguing and let him ride."

Clara came to her feet quickly. Hob noticed that she was looking to the south.

"He would have found us," Hob declared. "He would have seen our dust sign for miles."

Just then, Clara turned toward her husband. Tears flooded down her cheeks. "I . . . I know where he went, Tom," she said in a hoarse voice, crying openly now. "He went looking for Scoop. I should have guessed as much. He blamed himself for riding off and leaving the boy with Shorty and Soap."

Elena left her seat and hurried over to Clara, comforting her with an arm around her shoulder. "What is wrong, Senora Barclay?" she asked softly.

Clara slumped into Elena's arms. "Three of our men are missing over in Mexico," Clara cried, wiping tears from her cheeks. "One of them is hardly more than a child, a boy who lost his parents to an Indian attack. I've . . . looked after Scoop like a son. I know I must sound like a foolish old woman, but I've been so worried about him."

Elena cast a glance over her shoulder, questioning Hob with a look.

"It's a long story," Hob said, coming to his feet, eyeing the southern horizon. "It has to do with some buried money, a lot of money. Mr. Barclay can fill you in while I grab a change of clothes and a fresh horse. I've got to go after him. Mingus is my partner—and my friend."

"Hold on a minute, Hob," Tom replied, also standing now, with an eye to the south. "There are things we have to consider. Mingus has a two-day head start. You'll never catch up, and neither one of you knows where you're going. Those three men are lost somewhere in the Chisos; otherwise, we'd have heard from them by now. And remember that bounty hunter is down there, too, if Tip was right about the man's identity. I need you here at the ranch, Hob. I'll ask Tip if he'll go looking for Mingus and the others."

Hob was bristling when he answered Tom. "It's my responsibility. This whole thing is my fault, on account of me being fool enough to let my men go off on a wild-goose chase in the first place. I won't run the risk of putting Tip's neck in a noose for something I did. I'm going, Tom."

It was the first time Hob had ever bucked Tom Barclay over a decision, but his mind was made up. Tom stared at him, working the muscles in his cheeks.

"I know the Chisos," Don Miguel said, interrupting the conflict between Hob and Tom. "As a boy, I rode every foot of those mountains on a burro. Perhaps I can be of some help."

Both men faced Elena's father. Don Miguel's eyes went from Hob to Tom. "What part of the Chisos?" Don Miguel asked.

"Just below the river," Hob replied. "East of Ojinaga. The men have a letter that describes a canyon where a big cache of stolen money is buried in a cave beside a spring. We found the letter in a dead man's boot. Somebody hung him. We figure he was one of the bank robbers who stole the money, judging by what the letter had to say. I let the men have a couple of days off to see if they could find the right canyon. And the money."

Don Miguel stroked his gray beard thoughtfully. "A spring, you say? That would make the task much easier, senor. There are only a couple of springs in the northern Chisos on the Mexican side. One is called Agua Frio; the water is cold, even in the heat of summer. There is another, much deeper in the mountains, a very small spring known only to Yaqui goatherders and bandit gangs. Perhaps it is this spring your men are seeking?"

Hob approached the old man, searching his face. "Can you tell me how to find these springs?"

Don Miguel shook his head quickly. "Not if you do not know the Chisos, senor. The springs are well hidden in remote canyons. There are no trails. No one lives in those mountains, my friend. There is no grass for cattle, only the agave and lecheguia for the goats."

"Damn," Hob said, forgetting the presence of the women. "I have to make the try, Senor Montoya. Tell me as best you can how to find those springs."

Don Miguel glanced toward his daughter, then back to Hob. "Perhaps I can do better, senor. Perhaps Senor Barclay will make the loan of a horse, so I can show you the way to the place you seek?"

"Too dangerous," Tom protested. "You haven't heard the whole story, Senor Montoya. There's a paid killer down there, too, tracking my men in and out of those canyons. You'd be risking your life."

It seemed that the old man's eyes twinkled when he looked from one man to the other, and Hob wondered where Don Miguel saw any humor in what Tom told him.

"I have survived the murderous Yaquis and the Tarahumara," he said. "One man alone in the Chisos does not frighten me. Those are my mountains, senors, and I too have a rifle. If you will lend me a horse, I will show you the way."

Hob saw it as the best chance to find the missing Bar B cowboys. The old man knew the mountains. He could take Hob to the right canyons and save valuable time. "I'd appreciate the help, Senor Montoya," Hob answered, looking toward Tom for approval.

"You've got the loan of a horse," Tom said, shrugging. "Hob, tell Sancho to saddle an extra horse for Don Miguel, and have Cookie saddle a packhorse with the food you'll need."

Hob turned and started for the barn. "I'll need a few minutes to get the caliche washed off and change clothes," he said, glancing over his shoulder, catching Elena's eye as he hurried toward the gate.

By the time he reached the bunkhouse he was running, making a racket with his spur rowels. "Saddle two horses," he cried when he entered the door and found Sancho. "Tell Cookie to rig a packhorse with enough grub for a couple of weeks, just in case."

"What the hell's going on?" Tip asked, coming off his bunk, questioning Hob.

Hob grabbed his warbag from its peg on the bunkhouse wall. "Mingus took off for Mexico yesterday. He's gone after Scoop and the boys. I'm going after him."

"Count me in," Tip said, wheeling toward his gunbelt at the foot of his bed.

Hob halted near the door and shook his head. "You're stayin', and that's an order. This is my mess, and I'll clean it up myself."

Hob ran for the barn, to the big stone trough used for a bathtub by the men. He was half naked when Tom rounded the barn, headed for the trough with a look on his face that told Hob there was something on his mind.

"Saddle one more horse and take an extra bedroll," Tom said, exasperation in his voice, his cheeks an angry red. "Don

Miguel's daughter is going with you. I know it ain't proper, Hob, but the old man said to saddle another horse."

Hob pulled off his socks and stepped gingerly into the cold water with a bar of lye soap. "The woman's just going to get in the way. She'll slow us down, and if there's any gunplay she could get herself killed."

Tom shrugged. "I know, but it was Don Miguel's decision. They argued for a while in Spanish. Sounds like the woman's tongue was sharper than his. Anyway, be careful, Hob. Find Mingus first. If you get the opportunity, find Scoop and bring him back."

The boss left, and Hob faced the shard of mirror resting atop the stones at one corner of the trough, scraping whiskers from his chin with his razor. "Damn the luck," he said, thinking about Elena and the rough country they faced below the border. "She'll only be in the way."

When he was bathed and dressed in clean clothing, he hurried to the barn to inspect the saddling. Sancho had picked a big gray gelding for Hob's saddle and a rangy bay for Don Miguel. A buttermilk roan bore the packsaddle. "Saddle one more . . . something gentle enough for a woman to ride," he said, "and pack another bedroll." Hob circled the horses and headed for the saddle shed where the rifles were kept.

He selected a Winchester and two boxes of shells, then a rifle boot for his saddle. Cookie rounded a corner into the barn carrying a bag of hot biscuits to tie on the packhorse.

"Filled four extra canteens," Cookie announced, pointing to the packs tied to the roan. "It'll be dry below that river, Hob. Be damn careful you don't run out of water. Sancho took time to pick out the best horses for rough country. Keep your eyes peeled, and get yourself back in one piece."

Hob acknowledged Cookie's warning as he tied the rifle boot to his saddle. Just then, Tip entered the barn wearing his gun. By the look on his face, Hob judged the cowboy was set to make more argument for riding along.

"You're stayin'," Hob declared.

Tip's black eyes flashed with anger. "Scoop is my partner, Hob. It don't seem right that I have to stay."

"Right or wrong, that's the way it's gonna be. You're in charge of things while I'm away."

Tip's argument ended when Don Miguel and Elena entered the shaded hallway of the barn. Elena smiled at Hob, yet Hob hardly noticed, distracted as he was by the gunbelt around her waist.

"You're wearin' a gun," Hob sputtered.

"I can shoot it, Senor Shedd," she insisted, still smiling.

Hob let his shoulders drop. "I just hope you can aim with it," he said softly.

Elena's smile disappeared. Her cheeks colored. "I can shoot the eye of a rattlesnake at fifty paces," she snapped.

Hob spread his palms to apologize. "Sorry. Didn't mean to say the wrong thing. Sancho is saddling a horse for you," he muttered, looking the other way.

Don Miguel tied his rifle to the bay's saddle. Hob noticed that the gun was an old Spencer, gleaming with a layer of oil. Then the old man hung his warbag from the saddle.

"We are ready to ride when you are, senor," he said, pulling his big sombrero over his face to keep the sun from his eyes.

Sancho hurried toward the barn leading a sorrel mare, a mare Clara Barclay rode on her infrequent visits to the pastures with her husband. Sancho then cinched a saddle to the mare, helping Elena tie her belongings behind the cantle.

Hob led his gray from the barn and swung in the saddle, taking the lead rope on the packhorse from Cookie. "Let's ride," he said, watching Elena step expertly aboard the mare. "We'll see if we can pick up my partner's tracks when we get clear of the mouth of the canyon. My guess is Mingus will head for that cottonwood tree beside the river where we found the dead man. He'll start south into Mexico from the spot where Dave Cobb meant to cross the Rio Grande."

Don Miguel trotted his horse alongside Hob. Elena rode at her father's side, not looking at Hob, still angry over the remark he made about the gun. "Tell us about this letter," Don Miguel began, sighting the horizon. "Tell me everything you can remember about the description of the spring."

Hob recalled the letter as best he could, the grave where Jack was buried, and the cave where the money was hidden. Once, in the middle of his story, he found Elena sneaking glances his way, but when their eyes met she quickly turned her head. *Off to a bad start,* he thought, remembering the fire in Elena's eyes when he made mention of her gunbelt. *Stuck your foot in your mouth, didn't you, Mr. Shedd?*

CHAPTER 13

HOB tried to keep his mind on the task at hand. The woman was an unwanted distraction. It rankled him that Elena had come along in the first place, considering the risks. They would be riding through some of the wildest country in creation, headed for a canyon where a bounty hunter stalked three hapless cowboys who possessed a waybill to a fortune in stolen money. And a Texas Ranger lurked somewhere in the mountains, a man with a shadowy purpose who ignored the boundary between Texas and Mexico to look for the money. One of the men was a cold-blooded bushwhacker who put the bullet in Mingus's arm. One was the hangman who had ended Dave Cobb's life on the banks of the Rio Grande, when Cobb wouldn't tell him where the stolen money was buried. Hob and Don Miguel and Elena could be headed toward a deadly cross fire down in Mexico, and there was the chance of running across the Comanches who had waylaid Hob and Mingus in the mountain pass.

Considering all this as they followed Mingus's tracks, Hob found himself in a black mood. Protecting the woman was an obligation, should trouble start. It was the last thing he needed, to have a helpless female along to get in the way. Although she wore a gun and laid claim to being able to use it, Hob knew the woman would get them in trouble—trouble they didn't need.

They rode higher into the foothills, following the wagon road. Hob worried about Indians, sweeping the landscape for moving shadows as the sun lowered in front of them. Don Miguel and his daughter rode in silence, making their own study of the hills as purple shadows painted the rocky slopes and twisting gullies. Now and then the old man would turn his gaze to the south, toward the dim outlines of the Chisos below the border. When Hob described the canyon where the money was buried, Don Miguel shook his head thoughtfully. Hob wondered if the old man remembered the springs hidden deep in the mountains, after so many years. He claimed to know how to reach them. Hob silently hoped Senor Montoya's memory was good.

At dusk they crossed a rocky ridge where Don Miguel signaled a halt. He stood in his stirrups, staring at the purple shapes of the Chisos.

"What is it?" Hob asked.

"There," Don Miguel said, pointing south. "The big mountain is called El Diablo. We can save time riding toward this mountain."

Hob didn't like the idea. "We'll lose Mingus if we don't follow his tracks. He was acting a fool to ride off on his own in the first place, but he's my partner. We've got to find him first. I'm betting he'll cross the river where we found the dead man."

Don Miguel shrugged. "Suit yourself, my friend, but the shortest ride to the canyon you seek is this way, toward El Diablo."

Hob fidgeted. It was the way of things, to get complicated when you need them to be simple. Faced with a choice he did not want to make, he stared at the distant mountain.

"If your partner keeps riding his horse so hard," Elena remarked, pointing to the hoofprints, "we will never catch up with him. Perhaps my father's plan will allow us to cross his trail when he turns south?"

Hob turned to the woman, irritated by the objection she raised to his idea. But when he saw her face in the soft light, his anger dissolved. Her remarkable beauty had a strange effect on him, one he was powerless to explain just then. When he looked at her dark chocolate eyes his knees turned to jelly and his heart beat faster. Hob looked back toward the mountain. "I reckon your plan will save us some time," he said quietly. "It'll be easier on the horses."

He touched a spur to the gray's flank and reined south, leading the packhorse off the wagon ruts. Don Miguel and Elena fell in behind him for the ride across open country. Swinging wide of the cactus and yucca spines, they rode into the twilight shadows, listening to the rattle of horseshoes on rock. A quail darted from the path of the horses. Hob kept an eye peeled for night-feeding rattlesnakes as he contemplated the choice he'd made. Mingus was alone in a hostile land, still recovering from his wound. He would make easy prey for the Comanches if they were wandering the plains and hills below the river, one man against the nine Yamps who survived the battle in the mountain pass. One Winchester was missing from the rifle rack in the saddle shed. The repeater would be a help if Mingus encountered the Indians. "I hope I haven't hung you out to dry, partner," Hob whispered, guiding his gray between the mesquites and cactus thorns. "You were a damn fool to ride off alone, Mr. Strawn."

They crossed the river sometime after midnight, riding through belly-deep water in the deepest spots. When they rode out on the Mexican side of the Rio Grande, Hob swung back to wait for the old man and the girl.

"It's too dark to see the mountain," Hob said, addressing Don Miguel. "Lead the way. I'll be right behind you."

Don Miguel nodded and spurred past Hob. Hob waited for the woman politely, so she could ride behind her father. Instead, she swung her mare alongside Hob and rode with him. Hob felt a lump in his throat, wondering why Elena chose to ride beside him.

"The air is much cooler at night," she said. Her tone was friendly, and when Hob looked at her, he saw her smile.

"Easier on the horses," Hob added, making conversation.

"Your work . . . it must be very hard," she continued. "The

rancho of Senor Barclay is very big, like ours. A big rancho is a lonely place."

"A man can get lonesome," Hob agreed, questioning his good fortune with the woman so close beside him, asking about his work. His dark mood disappeared quickly. "Me and the boys look forward to the times when we ride over to Ojinaga."

Elena laughed. "So you can sleep with the *putas* and drink tequila?" she asked.

"Not exactly," he said, embarrassed. "Just havin' a little fun. There's no place else where a feller can meet a woman in these parts; a man needs himself a woman from time to time." Hob was grateful for the dark; Elena wouldn't see his ears turn red. She talked about such private matters as easily as another cowhand, but Hob squirmed in his saddle, wishing for a way to change the subject.

"Perhaps in the fall, when your work is finished, you will visit us?" Elena asked.

"Yeah. Sure. I was sorta planning on it, if you don't mind," he replied quietly.

"I will be looking forward to it," she said, and he saw her lips parted in a grin when she said it.

"So will I. In the fall, when we've taken the steers to the railhead," he said, his belly twisted in knots and his mouth dry.

He glimpsed Don Miguel's shadow when the old man turned around in the saddle. Finding Hob and Elena riding side by side, he slowed his horse and then spoke to his daughter. "Be silent, my child," he whispered. "This is dangerous land. Your silly chattering can wait for another time."

Sunrise was a welcome sight. The night ride had passed without incident, bringing them many miles closer to the peaks. Hob rode up beside Don Miguel to study the landscape, squinting into the morning haze.

"El Diablo," the old man observed, pointing to the tallest

mountain in their path. "It deserves its name. Only the devil himself can make it to the top."

Hob examined every foot of the rolling plain they would cross to reach the mountains, searching for a glimpse of a horse and rider. He saw no sign of a living soul in the empty desert. The chances of finding Mingus so soon were slim, what with his having a head start, but Hob was determined to look carefully anyway.

"We'll give our horses some grain and fix breakfast when we come to a shady spot," he id, nudging the gray toward Devil's Mountain. Hob took the front of their procession with the packhorse. Don Miguel brought up the rear as they entered a stretch of yucca flats leading to the foothills of the Chisos.

At midmorning, they rode up the first of many switchbacks where slender mesquites swayed in a gentle wind drifting down from the rocky slopes. Hob found a faint game trail running south where javelina and foraging armadillo had worn a pathway through the foothills. As the sun moved overhead, the heat grew until the horses broke into a lather. Bare patches of yellow caliche soil were powder dry between stretches of rock. Hardy cactus and agave grew in scattered clumps where the thin soil provided a meager foothold for the roots. The climb steepened as they wound their way steadily into the silent Chisos. Hob kept an eye on the slopes to the west, hoping for a glimpse of a lone horseman in the distance. And each time, he found nothing.

They rested in the shade of a rocky ledge to make coffee and eat biscuits and jerky, loosening the cinches on their winded horses while the coffee boiled. Hob studied the western slopes, chewing jerky, thinking about Mingus. When Elena walked up beside him he was lost in old memories, remembering times when he and Mingus rode the Santiagos together.

"You are worried about your friend," Elena remarked, shading her eyes from the sun to see the mountains.

"I reckon I am." Hob sighed. "We've been partners for a number of years. It's fair to say he's the best friend I ever had."

"Perhaps we will find him soon, Senor Shedd. Trust my father. He knows these mountains."

Hob shook his head to say he understood. Then he felt the woman's hand on his arm. When he looked at her, he saw genuine concern in her eyes. "Mingus will be okay," Hob said. "He knows how to take care of himself."

She squeezed his arm gently and let her hand drop. "Our coffee is ready, senor."

Hob grinned. "Call me Hob. Senor sounds too fancy."

"Then you must call me Elena," she replied. "Come. The coffee is finished, and my father grows impatient to be on our way."

They ate biscuits and drank coffee, squatting in the shade of the overhang. Hob doused the fire and tied the food on the buttermilk roan's packsaddle when the meal was done. While he cinched the saddles Don Miguel and Elena talked quietly, just out of earshot.

"Let's ride," he said, swinging a leg over the gray.

Don Miguel came over to Hob and aimed a finger. "Ride to the base of El Diablo. Follow the gullies. It will be easier on our animals, and there is a chance we may find a seep in the sand where we can dig water . . . enough to satisfy the horses. It will be much drier farther to the south. We must spare the horses all we can."

Following a gentle slope, they rode down from the ridge to a twisting wash that would take them southwest, toward El Diablo. Hob kept the gray in a walk, seeking the softest ground for the horse's hooves where he could find it. Here and there, in a bend in the wash, they encountered potholes littered with stones. But there was no water hidden in the rocks. Hob had never seen country so dry.

They rode into the shadow of the mountain late in the afternoon, as the sun lowered behind the craggy peak. Don

Miguel studied the ground briefly, then pointed due south. "That way," he said. "We will find a second gulley in an hour or two. Follow it. We must find water soon. The animals are suffering in this heat."

Hob's gray had begun to falter when they crossed rough ground, weakened by the heat and the climb. He wondered how the three Bar B men had fared when they rode these same dry mountains. "Hope they've still got their horses," he said to himself. "A man on foot out here is as good as dead."

So many weeks had passed since they began their search for the buried money. He told himself the odds were against them unless they found the spring described in the letter. Even then, with the bounty hunter John Frank Brown on their trail, the chances were slim that his friends were still alive. If they found the money, the bounty hunter would kill them for it. And if they didn't, the dry Chisos would kill them just as surely as a killer's bullet. One by one, their horses would die of thirst, and so would the men.

Hob, Don Miguel, and Elena rode south along the base of El Diablo, passing only a handful of places where sparse grasses grew. Hob halted their procession long enough to allow the horses to graze on the meager grass, then he pushed on, leaving the shadow of the mountain to ride more of the same barren waste.

At dusk, they rode into the gulley Don Miguel described, easing their tired horses down the steep embankment. The gulley was bone dry, as Hob expected. Don Miguel rode up beside Hob, looking southwest, following the course of the dry streambed with his eyes.

"This way," Don Miguel said, urging his weary bay to the front. "I know a spot where the sand is very deep. It was long ago, but when I was a boy herding goats in these mountains, I saved my goats from certain death when I dug a hole in the sand and found water. It is not far."

The horses plodded along the streambed as twilight became full dark. A handful of stars lighted their way. Once,

Hob looked over to Elena. She was slumped in her saddle, as weary as the mare she rode. When she saw Hob staring at her, she licked her parched lips and smiled.

"Are you okay?" he asked softly, offering her his canteen.

She shook her head, refusing the water. "I have ridden the deserts of Mexico all my life, Senor Shedd. Save the water—tomorrow, the canyons will be even drier."

He returned the canteen to his saddle horn, admiring Elena's spunk. She was proving that she was as tough as any cowhand, something Hob had never known a woman to be. The few women he'd known in his lifetime were mewing creatures in sunbonnets and flowing dresses. Elena Montoya was different.

They followed the wash for two hours, until a sliver of moon appeared above the dark outlines of the peaks around them. Here and there they rode through stretches of deep sand in the streambed where the old man would pause to examine a particular spot. Once, he got off his horse to dig with his hands, then he shook his head and mounted again without offering an explanation.

Hob guessed it was midnight as they rounded a bend in the wash and Don Miguel spurred his horse to a lope. The bay galloped around a turn, and Hob lost sight of him.

When Hob and Elena rounded the bend they found the old man on his knees, digging furiously beside a jumble of big rocks.

"Water," he said as they dismounted. "Help me dig."

Hob knelt and cleared sand from the hole. The sand felt wet on his fingertips. As the sand was cleared away, water seeped into the deepening hole.

"I'd have never thought to look here," Hob said, pawing wet sand from the hole as fast as he could. The horses scented the water. Elena's mare nickered, pawing the ground with a forefoot.

In a few minutes the pothole was elbow-deep, filling slowly with water. "Bring one animal and let it drink," Don Miguel said. "The hole will fill again when it is empty. It will take time, but the horses will have their drink and we can fill our canteens."

Hob stood up to survey his work while Elena brought her mare to the water. The horse drank noisily, sucking water through its muzzle until the hole was empty. Elena led her mare away. Hob leaned over to inspect the pothole in the moonlight. Fresh water seeped from the sand. "I'll be damned," he said, under his breath so the others couldn't hear him. "Learned a new trick."

It required an hour to water all the animals and fill the canteens. "We'll camp here tonight," Hob suggested, taking a look at their surroundings. "In the morning, we can water our mounts again. I sure hope Mingus found a pothole for his bronc. Otherwise, he'll be walking before the sun goes down tomorrow night."

Don Miguel grunted, sweeping the mountains with a careful look. "It is a dry year, *compadre*." He sighed. "If your friend is lucky, maybe he can find a handful of water hidden in the rocks."

Hob remembered his partner's four-leaf clover in the little jelly jar he carried in his saddlebags. Mingus believed the withered greenery brought him good luck, no matter what the evidence to the contrary might be. "Mingus brings along a good-luck charm," Hob replied, grinning when he thought about his friend. "He'll make it. Lady Luck is with him. Most of the time, she is."

Hob selected a spot in the sand for their bedrolls. He led the horses out of the wash and hobbled them where he could find patches of grass, stripping their saddles and bridles when he had them near grazing. Don Miguel built a fire of dead mesquite limbs, and Elena put coffee on to boil as Hob went about his chores. In short order their camp was prepared for the night. Off in the distance, a coyote howled at the moon. Hob came to the fire and took a tin cup, settling across the flames from Elena. In the flickering firelight, her face was as beautiful as ever and her dark eyes sparkled with reflected glow from the fire's embers.

"How is it such a pretty lady doesn't have a husband?" he asked, summoning his nerve to ask the question.

It was her father who answered Hob. "She has not met a man who is worthy of her," Don Miguel replied, filling his voice with an unmistakable warning. "My daughter will marry a fine young caballero one day, a gentleman. All others will be turned away."

Hob glanced across the flames. Elena lowered her eyes when he looked at her. "It is my father's right to choose my husband," she whispered. "It is the way of my people. It is our custom."

Hob felt the old man staring at him. "I understand. I was just curious."

The silence grew heavy around the campfire, until Hob got up to pass the sack containing the biscuits and jerky. They ate their meal without conversation, listening to the hiss and pop of the flames. Later, Hob spread his bedroll on the sand and rested his head against his saddle. Don Miguel and his daughter retired to their blankets.

"Good night, Hob," Elena whispered when the sounds of Don Miguel's snoring echoed in the wash.

"Good night," Hob answered. He drifted toward sleep with a smile on his face, hidden beneath his hat brim.

At dawn, they were under way. The pothole had given enough water to fill the horses' bellies before sunrise. Don Miguel led the way, spurring out of the sandy wash when he came to a gentle climb.

They rode through the stark Chisos until noon, once sighting a family of wild javelina pigs at the mouth of a tiny box canyon. Hob had never seen a place so empty. Not once did they cross a cattle track or a hoofprint. As the day wore on, he worried again about Mingus. It would take more than luck to bring Mingus through these same mountains without incident. If his horse did not die of thirst, Mingus could easily get lost in the monotonous sameness of the Chisos. Without Don Miguel Montoya leading the way, Hob himself would have been lost and would have died when his food supplies ran out and his canteens were empty.

CHAPTER 14

THE road seemed out of place. Since they crossed the Rio Grande, there had been no signs of habitation, and when they discovered the faint ruts crossing their path, Hob's spirits lifted.

"It has not been used for many years," Don Miguel said, pointing down to the ravine where the old wagon road passed in front of them. "A goatherd told me it was the route of the padres when they brought their gold and silver from the mines in the west to the waiting ships from Spain. The riches were carried in donkey carts, guarded by soldiers. It was a long time ago that the Franciscans worked the mines in the mountains. See how the weeds and grasses grow in the wagon tracks. No one has followed this road for a very long time. But we will follow it now, for it will lead us to the spring known as Agua Frio. Come. We are very close. Only a few hours more."

The old man sent his horse down the slope, turning east when he hit the bottom of the ravine. The sun baked the rocks around them as they rode down the ancient wagon road toward the spring Don Miguel remembered.

The ruts turned southeast, wandering through the Chisos. In places the road disappeared, swept away by time and lack of use, only to reappear again on the next gentle rise. Off in the distance, the ruts were faint scars following the course of a ravine to the next gradual climb. "Donkey carts and soldiers would need water," Hob reasoned aloud, guiding his gray along the road. "Maybe the old man is right. This road will take us to a spring."

Hob was concentrating on the land in front of them when he heard Elena call him. "Look, Hob!" she cried.

She was down from her mare, kneeling beside one of the ruts, when he reached her. Hob swung down to examine the ground where Elena was tracing a finger over a hoofprint.

"Shod horses," he said. "Two of them. The edges are rounded, maybe a week old."

Then he found a man's boot print farther down the ruts on a patch of barren caliche. "One of them is walking. He's lost his horse. Look at the front of this hoofprint. . . . The horse is dragging its hooves like it was lame, or weak from hunger and thirst. These could be the tracks of my men. It would make sense that they would follow this old wagon road, knowing it had to take them somewhere."

Don Miguel frowned down at the tracks from the back of his horse. "Perhaps they are the tracks of your friends," he said, twisting in his saddle to look southeast again. "If we hurry, we can make the spring before nightfall."

They rode off at a trot, pushing trail-weary horses into the heat with hopes of reaching the spring before dark. Hob studied the horizon, wondering about the bounty hunter. If John Frank Brown had been following the three cowboys, he most likely would have stayed on higher ground and kept his distance. It was a good bet that somewhere on the slopes above the wagon road, another set of hoofprints flanked the ravine.

A couple of hours before sunset the road swung sharply to the west, toward the mouth of a canyon. Steep rock cliffs jutted from the canyon floor on both sides, forming a narrow passageway. Hob slowed his horse as they neared the entrance, giving the rim of the canyon a careful look.

"Here's where it'll pay to be cautious," Hob said, pulling his .44/.40 to check the loads.

The old man drew his Spencer from the rifle boot. "The spring will be at the back of the canyon," he said. "The canyon turns south. If there is anyone in the canyon, they will see us when we ride through that opening."

"I'll go first," Hob declared. "The two of you wait here until I give a signal that it's clear."

Hob spurred the gray toward the canyon. "Be careful, Hob," he heard Elena say as the gray trotted into the mouth of the passageway.

For a hundred yards or more he rode between steep cliffs, listening to the rattle of the horse's iron shoes. The passage widened as he rounded a turn. Hob slowed the gray and tightened his grip on his Colt.

The passageway opened into a box canyon. The faint wagon ruts ran straight across the canyon floor toward a stand of drooping willow trees. Hob jerked his horse to a halt when he saw the carcass of an animal beside the glistening surface of a spring pool. Hob swung a look around him, watching the rim above the canyon, then heeled the gray toward the spring.

He approached cautiously, sighting the burned-out remains of a campfire beneath the willows. The gray snorted when it caught scent of the carcass. The horse still carried a saddle where it lay a few yards from the spring. The dead animal was bloated by the heat, but Hob found the Bar B brand on its flank when he stepped off the gray for a closer look.

Shorty's bay, he thought. *Got too weak to carry a rider. Probably foundered on water when it got its belly full.*

He knelt to read the tracks around the pool. Hoofprints and boot tracks covered the damp caliche near the edges of the tiny spring. He examined the sign for some time, trying to make some sense of the confusion, until he heard horses approach the trees from the mouth of the canyon.

Don Miguel and Elena rode up beside him. "We found their tracks when they left the canyon," Don Miguel said. "Three men on foot, leading a single animal."

"Which way did they go?" Hob asked.

"Southeast, following the old road. The next spring is two days farther into the mountains. I suspect your friends were headed toward it when they left Agua Frio."

Hob examined the canyon carefully. There was no cave in the canyon walls, and no grave marker described in the letter. "The wrong canyon, and the wrong spring," he said. "Appears they were too fool-headed to give up searching for the money. I reckon they figured they'd come this far, so they might as well go the rest of the way. They used up their horses, riding all over these mountains. Looks like they were down to just one by the time they left here. At least the three of them were still alive when they found this spot."

Hob thought about Mingus when he looked north, toward the canyon rim. "I hope Mingus had the sense to spare his horse all he could. We gambled wrong, figuring to cut his trail when we aimed for El Diablo. We could ride our horses into the ground, looking for him in this wasteland. About the best we can do is push on, and hope for a bit of luck."

It was Elena who offered the first bit of hopeful news. "If your partner knows dry country, he will follow the flight of the birds at sunset. They will lead him toward water."

Hob shook his head. "I doubt if Mingus knows such a trick. He's never been out in a desert like this by his lonesome. He grew up around a place called Fort Smith, up in Arkansas, where water's never a problem."

Don Miguel swung down to examine the tracks at the edge of the pool before he permitted his horse a drink. "Two more horses have come to the spring," he said, pointing across the pool to scattered tracks and boot prints. "One man, and two horses."

"The bounty hunter." Hob sighed, remembering that whoever had hanged Dave Cobb had taken his horse when he crossed the Rio Grande. "John Frank Brown has a spare mount. I reckon those tracks are his. Let's water our horses and get moving down the tracks quick as we can. I hope we're not too late. This sign is a week old. Maybe older."

They led their horses to the pool. Hob filled their canteens and passed around strips of jerky. All the while he was thinking about Mingus's plight in the dry mountains north of the canyon. "We never should have left his trail," he muttered under his breath.

Don Miguel was examining the campsite beneath the willows while Hob was busy with the canteens. Elena knelt on a rock at the edge of the pool, washing her face and arms with a cloth.

"Your friends killed a wild pig," Don Miguel said, pointing to a crude spit above the ashes of the camp fire. "They have food and water. If they followed the tracks of the burro carts, they have reached the next spring. They have only one horse, so they must travel slowly."

Hob was looking at the tracks of the bounty hunter as Don Miguel spoke. "It's the next spring that I'm worried about," he said, following the hoofprints with his eyes where they left the spring pool. "That'll be where John Frank Brown tries to jump them, if they've found the buried money. Not one of my men is any great shakes with a gun."

Hob tightened the cinch on the gray and swung in the saddle. He gave the box canyon a final look, then reined toward the opening with Don Miguel and the woman trotting beside him.

When they were away from the mouth of the canyon, Hob saw the bounty hunter's tracks, off to one side of the wagon ruts.

"He's right on their trail," Hob said, hurrying the gray as much as he dared in the late-day heat.

The sun dropped below the mountains. Hob worried about riding into an ambush in the dark. The road twisted through countless tight places where a bushwhacker could hide himself for a shot at close range. The sounds of their horses would alert the gunman. Hob could be leading Don Miguel and Elena into a trap.

Around midnight, they stopped to rest their horses and

spread their bedrolls for a few hours of sleep. They camped in a shallow draw to one side of the trail, not risking a fire. At first, Hob was too edgy to close his eyes. He sat on his blankets, watching the stars, thinking about Mingus and the Bar B men, until Don Miguel began snoring. Just as Hob stretched out against his saddle, he heard the woman stirring in the darkness.

She came over and sat beside him, pulling her hair away from her face. He sat up, quickly glancing around him once to be sure Elena's father was asleep.

"You are worried about your friends," she whispered, a statement rather than a question.

"I feel responsible," he replied softly, toying with a blade of grass. "I let them go in the first place."

She touched his arm, and her touch brought a tingle to his skin. "Don't blame yourself, Hob. They must have understood the danger."

He shook his head, unnerved by Elena's closeness. "I reckon they did, 'cept for the boy."

She squeezed his arm gently. "On the outside, you act like a gruff vaquero. But I see a soft heart inside you. You carry the blame for your friends' misfortune. It surprises me to discover that you are a gentle man who cares so much about his friends."

They stared into each other's eyes. Hob felt a flutter in the pit of his stomach. He wondered if he might be falling in love with Elena, although he had no experience by which he could judge the feeling. "You are a beautiful lady," he whispered hoarsely, surprising himself when the words left his mouth.

Elena smiled, then leaned closer and gave him a gentle kiss. It was the lightest of touches, not really a kiss by Hob's measurement, for their lips had only brushed together briefly.

"That . . . was nice," Hob stammered as his heartbeat

quickened. "I'm not exactly sure how a man is supposed to act when he gets kissed by a proper lady."

She answered him by placing her arms around his neck. "It is proper to return a woman's kiss, if your feelings are the same toward the woman," she whispered.

Slowly, carefully, he leaned forward and placed his lips against her mouth. Kissing Elena's lips was akin to touching the petals of a wildflower in the high mountain meadows in early spring, being careful not to crush the flower in his work-hardened hands. Picking flowers was something he did when he was alone, when no one else was watching, not even his best friend Mingus. He was thankful that no one was watching him now, as Elena allowed her lips to linger against his. Then she pulled away very slowly, staring into his face.

"From the very first moment I saw you, I felt something pass between us," she whispered. "I can't explain it properly . . . we were strangers. Nothing like this has ever happened to me before."

Hob swallowed, gently pushing a stray lock of hair from her forehead with a fingertip. "You're the prettiest lady I ever met, Elena." He sighed, words spilling from his mouth now. "I don't reckon I ever figured I'd be lucky enough to kiss a woman like you."

She traced a finger along his cheek. "You are a handsome vaquero, Hob. My father has never allowed me to share the company of a man like you. He insists that I be escorted only by the sons of his wealthy friends, for among them he will choose who I must marry."

Hob glanced cautiously toward Don Miguel's bedroll. The old man slept peacefully. "It doesn't seem fair. If a man loves his daughter, he'd let her pick the man she wants to spend her time with."

Elena's eyes clouded. "He loves me . . . perhaps too much. He wants only what is best for me. It is his right to choose."

"Don't seem right," Hob whispered. He placed his hand under Elena's chin and lifted her face, then kissed her again as gently as he could. A soft breeze whispered down from the mountains, fluttering Elena's hair about her face.

She drew back when his kiss lingered, lowering her eyes the way Rosita did when she was being coy. "We must not wake my father," she said. "Good night, Hob. Do not worry about your friends. We will find them soon."

She was gone before he could think of the right thing to say, before he could wish her good night. He watched her snuggle into her blankets beneath the stars.

Her sudden departure left him with a terrible sense of longing. He wished for the chance to hold her in his arms a moment longer and to feel the warmth of her arms around his neck. The good feelings of moments before were replaced by feelings of despair.

"Just my luck," he told himself, resting his head against his saddle to stare at the heavens, "to fall for a woman I can't have. Her father would hang me up by my boots if he caught us together."

He stared at the sky for a time, remembering the feel of her lips and the warm sensation in his belly when she put her arms around him. Even though he was bone-tired from so many days and nights in a saddle, he could not drift off to sleep, tossing about on his bedroll, dozing fitfully.

He was thankful when the eastern sky brightened with false dawn, ending his soft recollections of Elena. When he pulled on his boots, he was as tired as he was before he lay down at midnight.

Dawn brought a crisp coolness to the mountains. Tiny drops of dew clung to the brittle agave leaves and cactus, sparkling in the morning sunlight. In only a few hours the heat would be unyielding again, until the day ended. But for the moment the horses traveled easily in the cooler air.

Hob surveyed the slopes around them as they rode out of the ravine. Somewhere in the mountains, a killer waited for his victims to lead him to a fortune in stolen bank loot. As Hob swung down the dim ruts made long ago by the burro carts, he prayed that he wasn't already too late to help his friends. And while he was at it, he asked the Almighty to look after Mingus.

Elena rode up beside him and Hob forgot about the dangers ahead, distracted by the woman's smiling face, remembering the way her lips felt when she kissed him.

"Are you feeling better?" she asked.

Hob glanced at Don Miguel to see if the old man was listening. "Worryin' some, I reckon. About my friends." The warmth of her smile made him forget a lot of things, though he had not entirely forgotten the threat in Don Miguel's voice when he had spoken of his plans for the future of his daughter.

Don Miguel turned back in the saddle when he overheard their remarks. He did not conceal the anger in his eyes when he noticed their apparent intimacy.

CHAPTER 15

THEY made camp at dusk, sheltered by a ledge where the old road crossed a dry streambed. They were exhausted by another long day spent in their saddles, so conversation was at a minimum when they ate a meal of cold biscuits and jerky.

"Tomorrow," Don Miguel said, pointing southeast. "Half a day, and we come to the spring."

"Time we rode careful," Hob replied. "At sunup, I ride out front. The two of you stay a safe distance behind. Just keep me in sight, but don't get too close. If there's gonna be trouble from the bounty hunter, it'll come tomorrow when we get close to that spring."

Don Miguel nodded thoughtfully. "There is another way to approach the canyon, if my memory does not betray me in my old age. There is a trail to the top of the canyon rim, where the Yaquis would post their lookouts for the soldiers. If I can find that trail, we can ride up to the top of the canyon."

Hob wasn't really listening to the old man, but was thinking about what tomorrow's sunrise might bring, wondering what they would find in the canyon. He would not allow himself to think about the chances of finding three dead bodies at the spring; he pushed the thought from his mind.

He hobbled the trail-weary horses and spread his bedroll. When he rested his head against his saddle, he thought fleetingly of Elena again. Would she come to him again in the darkness so they could share another stolen moment alone?

Before he was aware of it, the sleepless night and a dozen

hours in the saddle took its toll on him. He drifted into a hazy sleep and slept soundly until dawn.

He rolled out of his blankets, overcome by a sense of dread. Strapping on his gunbelt, he swung his gaze to the south. Somewhere beyond the empty mountains lay the answer to his friends' fate. A killer stalked those mountains. Hob hoped he wasn't already too late to take a hand in things.

Once, as he saddled their horses for the ride, he wondered what had become of the Ranger. Glancing around him, scanning the silent peaks, he thought about Carl Tumlinson. Was he waiting out there, too, for the chance to get his hands on the money?

More likely, things were settled in the canyon by now. Whoever had used the greater caution was already the owner of the robbery loot. Odds were that Hob was late by several days to be of any help to his friends. Thinking of it, Hob felt a knot form in the pit of his stomach.

They rode out after a bite of jerky. "Stay back now," Hob warned, spurring off at a lope to the crest of a switchback running between the slopes. Filled with a sense of foreboding, Hob hurried along the wagon ruts with his right hand resting on the butt on his gun.

It was an hour or so before noon when Hob spotted the canyon in the distance. The entrance was almost hidden, and only a careful eye would have found it without the telltale ruts of the donkey carts. Hob slowed the gray and studied the canyon rim on either side, then turned back to wave at Don Miguel and Elena to warn them off the road. But the trail behind him was empty. Don Miguel and Elena were nowhere in sight. "Must have found the trail to the top," he thought, urging his horse forward.

He rode toward the canyon, dreading what he would find. As he neared the entrance, his gray snorted once, sensing something in its path. Hob drew his Colt, sweeping the rocks above him as he rode closer. Had the horse heard a sound? he wondered.

He was a hundred yards from the narrow mouth of the canyon when the gray snorted again. Hob reined down and sat quietly to study the rocks above him. What was spooking the gray?

His answer was more of the same silence. "What is it, ol' boy?" he asked softly, knowing the horse could not tell him what he wanted to know. Was someone hidden up there on the rim? Or in the passageway, behind a rock?

Hob swung down, his mind made up to go the rest of the way on foot. The gray sensed something ahead of them in the trail. Every cowboy learned to trust his horse in wide-open spaces, for the animal had keener hearing and better eyesight than a man. On more than one occasion, Hob's horse had saved him from getting too close to trouble: a coiled rattlesnake, or a ledge where the scent of a mountain lion made the horse shy away.

He tied the gray's reins to a mesquite limb and pulled his Winchester from the saddle boot. He worked a shell into the chamber and then started off on foot, keeping to the protection of the trees as much as he could until he was near the mouth of the canyon. The silence of the place was eerie; there was only the rattle of his spurs as he drew near the rock-strewn passage. He crept along at a snail's pace, watching the rim and the rocks in his path, feeling sweat pour down his back and from his hatband. A step at a time, he entered the opening, crouching down when a rock offered protection from above. He waited for several minutes before he moved deeper into the passage, but he could find nothing amiss. What was it that had alerted the gray?

Using all the stealth he possessed, he crept between the rocks with the rifle aimed in front of him. Had his horse scented dead bodies in the canyon? Did that explain why the gray wanted to go no farther?

Slowly, he moved toward a widening of the canyon walls.

The canyon was smaller than the one they visited before, hardly more than a pocket in the barren rock mountains. Inching closer, he could make out the far wall of the canyon and the rim. Not a sound came from the enclosure, not so much as a whisper, or a distant footfall, or a breath of air.

The rock cliffs widened. Across the canyon floor, Hob could see a single stunted willow tree. He froze when he saw the carcass of a dead horse beside the tree. A bloated sorrel lay outstretched in the sparse shade beneath the limbs, with a saddle tied to its back. *They lost their last horse,* he thought, sweeping the rim before he advanced any closer. *I wonder if they're still alive? Why are things so quiet in here?*

He was unwilling to risk a shout to see if anyone answered his call. There was a chance his friends were hiding somewhere in the canyon, perhaps pinned down by rifle fire from the rim. Just then his thoughts drifted to Elena and her father. Had they found the trail that would take them to the top of the cliffs? Without an answer he crept forward, moving from one boulder to the next to keep from making a target of himself until he was in the canyon. He crouched down to examine the lay of things, taking in every detail as quickly as he could.

He spotted the dark opening of a cave beyond the spring, to Hob's left, perhaps two hundred yards away. "That's where I'll find them," he told himself. "Dead or alive, that's where they'll be . . . inside that cave."

He started across the canyon in a crouch, hunkered down to present as small a target as possible when he crossed open ground. Before he was twenty yards from the safety of the rocks, a sixth sense warned him of trouble.

"Look! It's Hob," someone shouted. Hob thought he recognized the voice, and its familiarity made him forget his caution. He straightened and started to call out to the voice from the cave. Suddenly, there was a booming gunshot, shattering the silence.

A stabbing, white-hot pain shot through his leg above his

knee. The force of the bullet knocked Hob off his feet; he went sprawling, face first, into the dirt. His rifle fell from his hands, and then gunshots exploded all around him.

He raised his head, blinking dust from his eyes, trying to collect himself. A bullet whacked into the dirt beside him, ricocheting off harmlessly. *I've got to get to that cave,* he thought quickly, deafened by the thunder of the guns.

He scrambled to his feet, wincing when his weight fell on his injured leg. A slug whistled past his face. He ducked when he felt the hot breath of wind, grabbing his Winchester before he took off in a limping run for the mouth of the cave.

Dirt spewed from the ground in front of him as a bullet went wide of its mark. Hob forced the injured leg to carry him faster. He floundered to the edge of the spring pool and fell when his boot stuck in the caliche mud.

"Help him," someone cried from the cave.

Hob looked up as he struggled to his hands and knees. A man ran toward him, crouching to avoid the flying lead. Scoop Singleton scurried over to the pool, his eyes walled white with fear. He grabbed Hob by his shirt collar and jerked him to his feet. "Run, Hob!" he shouted, then his glance fell to the blood flowing from Hob's leg.

They were off in a stumbling run toward the cave before Hob could clear his addled brain. Gunshots filled Hob's ears, and the crack of spent lead bounced from the rocks. Seconds later they went diving, face first, into the mouth of the cave. Hob landed on his belly; his rifle went clattering to the rocks as the wind rushed out of his lungs. Stray bullets ricocheted into the opening, singing a deadly song until they rattled harmlessly to the floor of the cave.

Hob rolled over on his back and shook his head, trying to clear the cobwebs. He saw Shorty Stewart crouched down near the opening with a pistol in his hands. Scoop was beside him, peering down at Hob's face when he tried to sit up. The gunfire ended abruptly, then Hob heard Soap Osborn's voice from the other side of the cave. "You okay, Hob?" he asked.

"My leg," Hob groaned, sitting up. He touched the wound above his knee, thankful to be alive. His denims were torn where the bullet grazed his thigh. The wound was bleeding, but not serious. The slug had passed clean through.

Soap came over to Hob, kneeling down to examine the leg. "It ain't too bad, Hob."

"I'll make it," Hob said, blinking when he stared out the opening into the bright sunlight. "Tell me what happened. We've been trailing you for days."

"There's a feller up there on the rim, keeping us holed up in the cave during the day. At night we can sneak out and get water, if we're real careful about it. We found that money, Hob. You oughta see it. I never saw so much money in all my born'd days. We're rich. All we've got to do is figure a way to get that bastard up on them rocks, afore he gets us . . . afore we starve ourselves to death."

While Soap was talking, he was tying his bandana around Hob's leg to stem the blood. Gradually, Hob's eyes adjusted to the dark inside the cave. When the knot was tied in the bandage, Hob took a look around. The tunnel ran quite a distance into the rock.

"We're mighty glad to see you, Hob," Scoop said, resting a hand on Hob's shoulder. The boy seemed older than Hob remembered.

"Thanks for coming out to get me . . . that was a brave thing you done. Hand me my rifle and help me get on my feet, so I can see what kind of a predicament we're in."

Scoop gave him the Winchester and helped him to stand. Hob peered out the opening, limping toward a pile of rocks where Shorty watched the canyon rim.

"Where is he?" Hob asked.

"Yonder," Shorty said, pointing with his gun barrel. "Right there in that niche. He keeps us penned up in here. A couple of days ago, we tried to slip out after it got dark, but he was wise to us. That's when he got the Ranger."

"The Ranger?" Hob asked. "You mean Carl Tumlinson is here?"

Shorty jerked a thumb over his shoulder. "He's layin' back there in the cave. Took a bullet in the chest when we were making the try to get out of the canyon. It's a long story, Hob. The Ranger was following our tracks. He found us whilst we were in here digging up that money, and got the drop on us. He had us figured for part of the outlaw gang that pulled off the robbery. We told him about the letter, and how we'd rode all over this part of Mexico looking for the loot. He said he'd met up with you over in Ojinaga, and after he found out who we were, he holstered his gun and told us the whole story. The Texas Rangers lost a good lawman back there. He died tryin' to get the bank its money when that bushwhacker shot him."

Hob let out a sigh. "I had him figured wrong. I thought he was after the loot to keep it for himself."

Hob moved closer to the mouth of the cave, hunkered down behind the rocks. The niche on the canyon rim gave the bounty hunter a clear view of the canyon floor. There was no way out of the canyon without passing under Brown's gun sights.

"Did you bring Mingus and some of the boys?" Soap asked, watching Hob's face intently.

Hob shook his head. "Mingus got himself shot by the same bushwhacker when we tried to follow you from Ojinaga. He's been laid up at the ranch. . . . Only, the other day, he took off on his own to look for the three of you while we were out rounding up the high-country herds. The springs went dry up in the mountains, and the boss man sent us to drive the cattle to the river. Right now I don't know where Mingus is, or if he's still alive."

"You mean you came by yourself?" Shorty asked softly, as if he didn't believe it.

Hob squinted along the rim, wondering about Elena and her father. "I came with an old Mexican rancher and his daughter. They knew these mountains. It was them that led me to this canyon. Without their help, I'd have never found you."

"Where are they now?" Shorty asked, peering up at the rocks.

"Out there somewhere. The old man knew another trail, and I reckon he took it."

Shorty shook his head. "That bastard will kill them both, Hob. He won't let nothin' stop him from getting his hands on this money. He's one hell of a good shot, whoever he is."

Hob settled against the rocks, trying to think of a way out of the trap they were in. "His name is John Frank Brown, and he's a bounty hunter from up north someplace. He rode in at the ranch a few weeks back, probably following Dave Cobb. It's my guess he's the gent who hung Cobb. All he wants is the money."

"Wait'll you see it, Hob," Shorty said. "That pile of loot is just about the prettiest sight I ever saw in my whole life."

Hob wheeled angrily toward Shorty. "Was it worth all this trouble?" he snapped. "It killed the Texas Ranger and might've got Mingus killed. You boys have been nothin' but a pack of damn fools, and the way things are sizing up just now, that money may cost every one of us our lives before it's over."

CHAPTER 16

Hob was worried about Elena and her father. He studied the rim, listening for the first telltale gunshot that would spell trouble. Waiting, he listened to Shorty and Soap as they filled him in on their wanderings through the mountains. It had been trial and error, according to their account of what led them to this canyon and the cave. One by one their horses had died of thirst and starvation, until they were down to the last animal, the sorrel killed by the bounty hunter when a hail of bullets started flying from the canyon rim. Ranger Carl Tumlinson had fared little better, losing his horse to a broken leg as he rode the high country above the wagon road, following from a distance until he was led to the cave and the missing money. The bounty hunter killed Tumlinson when they tried to leave the cave four days back, according to Shorty.

When Hob looked at his friends, he could see the effect of their ordeal on their haggard faces. For days they'd been trapped inside the tunnel, existing on handfuls of water and the last of the wild pig they shot at the spring called Agua Frio. Just thinking about the troubles the three men brought to the ranch made Hob angry enough to hang them up by their boots. It was greed, he decided, that kept them from turning back for the ranch when they couldn't find the money at first.

"You've been damn fools," he said. "There's no excuse that's good enough for what you've done. Right now, I've got to figure a way to get us out of here with our skins. Heading the list of our troubles is that bounty hunter, not to mention the fact that there ain't enough horses to go around if we can figure a way to get clear of this cave. We're in one hell of a fix, and we've got the three of you to thank for it."

The men were silent.

"I can't figure how that bounty hunter is getting water for himself and his horses," Hob whispered, talking to himself. His leg had stopped bleeding, and the pain had lessened.

"He slips down at night," Soap replied. "He leads his horses up behind that tree and fetches water in his hat. We can hear him, only we ain't been able to get a clean shot at him. We don't have a rifle, Hob. These pistols ain't accurate over the distance, but his rifle damn sure is. Can't see him good in the dark, either. He's got all the aces in his hand."

"Maybe things have changed," Hob said thoughtfully, taking a better grip on the stock of his Winchester. "Maybe the odds have swung our way tonight, when he comes down to get water. I only hope Don Miguel and Elena have the good sense to keep out of sight, so they don't get caught in the cross fire. I reckon we'll have to sit tight until it gets dark. The bounty hunter knows I have a rifle, so maybe he'll be extra careful showing himself."

"He's mighty slippery," Soap agreed. "He makes a feller think he's in one place, only he winds up bein' in another. We ain't got but a few shells left."

Shadows lengthened beyond the mouth of the cave. Now and then a bird would chirp from the limbs of the willow tree; otherwise the canyon was silent. Hob thought about his gray, tied to the mesquite outside the canyon. Horses were precious things now, so far from civilization. They could mean the difference between life and death if Hob and his men could get away from the trap they were in. The gray would have to have water soon, and so would the horses Don Miguel and Elena rode. But the only water within a day and half's ride was a hundred yards from the mouth of the cave, covered by the gun up above.

"The bounty hunter has to make the first move," Hob declared, considering the shape of things. "We have to be ready for him when he comes down from that niche. He'll have to ride out of sight, to come around to the mouth of the canyon. When he does, I aim to be waiting for him someplace else. Maybe I can catch him unawares."

Shorty shook his head. "He's a tricky bastard, Hob. I wouldn't count on taking him by surprise."

"I don't see how we've got much choice," Hob replied, taking another look around the canyon floor. "We can't just sit here and starve to death waiting for him to make a stupid move. We've got to try something."

Hob pulled off his boots before he crept to the mouth of the cave with his rifle. Peering into the darkness, he listened for the slightest sound and heard nothing. "All clear," he whispered to the men gathered around him. "Keep your guns ready, but don't waste a shot. And make damn sure of your target before you pull the trigger. There's an old man and a woman out there someplace. They heard all the shooting this afternoon, so I don't figure they'll show themselves. But just in case, remember they're out there. I brought that 'old buttermilk roan along to pack our gear. He'll be easy to see, even in the dark, so don't fire a shot if you see that ol' roan."

Hob crawled out on his belly, remembering things he learned as a boy among the Comanches. Keeping the rifle under his body so it would not reflect starlight, Hob edged forward from the mouth of the cave, holding his breath. Using only his elbows, he inched away from the tunnel, keeping to the cliff where the night shadows were the deepest and fallen rock from the rim offered some protection. He moved at a snail's pace, creeping forward only after long pauses. Twenty yards in front of him lay a boulder he could hide behind . . . if he could crawl the twenty yards without being killed. It required patience to crawl as slowly as he must, to avoid being seen from the rim. Hob knew the only way to elude the watchful bounty hunter was to make himself a part of the shadows beneath the cliff.

It seemed an eternity before he made the safety of the boulder. If he lay flat, the rock would hide him from the bounty hunter's bullets. He waited, catching his breath, surrounded by a silent darkness, listening for the distant scrape of a hoof. He had a clear view of the water hole. When the bounty hunter came for water, he would be in for a surprise.

Minutes stretched into hours as he waited behind the rock. His limbs grew stiff. All the while he thought about Elena and Don Miguel. The gunshots must have alerted them to the danger, because they had stayed out of sight. Still, they were out there someplace in the surrounding mountains, without water for their horses. Silently, Hob hoped they had found his gray and taken it away from the mouth of the canyon.

A distant sound distracted him from his thoughts. He listened closely and heard it a second time, coming from the passageway into the canyon. He strained to see movement in the shadows, but he saw nothing.

Then he heard the unmistakable scrape of a horseshoe and the soft *plop* of a shod hoof on hard ground. Slowly, he raised his rifle sights to the mouth of the canyon and waited.

Shadows moved in the opening. A man led two horses into the canyon, moving cautiously, a few steps at a time. Hob sighted in on the form of the man and held his breath.

The bounty hunter, he thought, following the dim outline with his gun barrel. "Wait 'til you're sure of the shot," he told himself, tightening his finger on the trigger.

The man approached carefully, keeping the tree between himself and the cave. He halted often to look and listen to his surroundings. Hob could see the gleam of a rifle in his hands.

Then the shadowy form walked quietly to the tree. He knelt and ground-hitched his horses, then crept toward the pool with his gun aimed in front of him. His boots made no sound on the caliche. It was as if he wore moccasins, like a Comanche.

He knelt again and pulled off his hat. Hob drew a bead on his chest as he caught water in the crown of his Stetson.

Now, Hob thought, tugging the trigger gently.

The Winchester slammed into Hob's shoulder and the roar of the gun filled the canyon. The man dove to one side, then Hob saw brilliant flashes of light as the bounty hunter's gun fired. Hot lead splattered against the boulder where Hob lay in hiding, kicking tiny fragments of rock into Hob's eyes. For a moment, Hob was blind.

Gunshots bellowed from the cave. Soap and Shorty fired their pistols, even though the range was too great for any accuracy. Hob sought his target with the Winchester as the gunman's horses spooked away from the rattle of gunfire.

"Missed him," Hob hissed savagely, knowing it could prove to be a fatal mistake. He saw the moving shadows of the frightened horses, but the shape of a man was not among them as they fought their hobbles to run away from the gunfire.

Hob levered another shell into the chamber and cursed his bad luck. He couldn't let Brown get back up on that rim—he had to go after him.

He came up in a crouch and ran for the tree, limping on his damaged leg, ignoring the pain. He swept the darkness with his gun and saw nothing to shoot at. Unaccountably, the bounty hunter had escaped in the melee.

Hob reached the tree trunk and hid behind it, panting from his run. The bounty hunter's horses reared awkwardly toward the passage in full flight, fighting the restraint of the hobbles as they lunged away from the pool. Suddenly, Hob saw a shape alongside the floundering horses. The gunman was between them, shielding himself from Hob's bullets. "Damn," Hob whispered, not daring to risk hitting one of the horses because they were the only hope he and the others had of making it back to Texas—assuming they could get the bounty hunter before he killed all of them.

Hob took a desperate chance: he raced away from the tree, crouching, dodging back and forth to make himself a difficult target in the dark. He followed the pair of horses with his gun sights aimed at the shadow between them. He ran for his life in spite of his crippled leg.

At one point, Hob stumbled, yet his resolve kept him on his feet after his quarry. The lunging horses disappeared around a bend in the passage. Hob ran straight for the cliff on bare feet without giving a thought to the sharp stones and thorns.

He made the safety of the wall and ran along it, staying low with his rifle ready. In the passageway it was too dark to see anything clearly, but he could hear the clatter of horseshoes as he hurried through the shadows.

The bounty hunter led the horses into a stand of mesquite trees. Hob followed. He could hear the horses and he turned toward the sound, slowing to a trot, being careful not to run blindly into an ambush. The trees blocked out even the meager starlight, so he trotted through a velvety curtain of black, guided by the sounds of the horses crashing through the limbs.

Suddenly there was a change in the hoofbeats. One horse struck a gallop, its hooves clattering over the rocks, fading away. Hob figured Brown had got the hobbles off one of the horses and was making a getaway.

He found the second animal in a clearing, still hobbled by its forelegs, snorting when Hob approached. "Easy boy," Hob said, reassuring the gelding with a hand across its muzzle.

He held the horse's reins while he knelt to pull off the hobbles. Then he swung on the animal's back and urged the horse to a trot, following the fading hoofbeats. Mesquite thorns tore his shirt as he rode through the limbs, hard on the trail of the gunman. "I can't lose him . . . not now," he said aloud, heeling the gelding to a lope.

The trail crisscrossed the ledge, leading higher up the mountain. A sheer rock face was to the left of the trail, and to the right a fathomless drop to a ravine. Hob kicked the horse to a lope and bent low over its neck, charging after the bounty hunter.

The gelding galloped over treacherous footing in an all-out run. Soon the horse was laboring for breath, weakened by the climb.

Hob drove his heels into the animal's sides, relentlessly after his quarry. Higher still, the trail bent sharply. A steeper climb followed the turn, by way of a narrow passage between slabs of slippery rock. Here, the gelding pawed for a purchase with its iron shoes, scrambling toward the top. Suddenly, the gelding stumbled and went down heavily, spilling Hob from its back as it crashed on its chest.

Hob toppled to the ground, clinging fiercely to his rifle. The gelding regained its footing and charged past him, trailing its reins. Hob ran for the horse the moment he got to his feet, but the horse galloped away from him, leaving Hob afoot on the starlit ridge.

A gunshot thundered from the darkness.

Hob lunged to one side and landed flat, trying to find the muzzle flash. Without taking aim, he squeezed off a shot. He was shooting blind, foolishly making an easy target of himself.

The clatter of shod horses echoed across the ledge. Hob aimed for the sound, when he heard the shrill cry of a woman's voice.

"Drop the gun!" Elena shouted.

The bounty hunter wheeled his horse and drew his aim on the direction of the warning. Hob quickly levered a shell into the chamber, but he was too late. As the bounty hunter fired, an answering gunshot came from the ledge. Hob saw the bounty hunter slump over his saddle. The horse whirled skittishly and the rider fell.

Hob ran toward the fallen bounty hunter.

"Be careful, Hob!" Elena cried from her hiding place on the ledge.

Too late, Hob saw the gleam of gunmetal in the moonlight as the bounty hunter raised his pistol. "Don't try it!" Hob yelled, aiming his rifle as he skidded to a halt.

Hearing the deadly click of a cocked hammer, Hob triggered off a shot. Brown's body jolted and fell back against the rock, then the pistol clattered as it fell from the gunman's hand.

The bounty hunter groaned. Hob's bullet had caught him in the chest, and now there was the wet sound of a bullet-torn lung as the gunman gasped for air. Hob lowered his rifle and knelt beside the dying man.

The bounty hunter looked up at Hob. Even in the pale light, Hob could make out the gunman's features. Slowly, Brown's mouth twisted into a snarl. "Did . . . they find . . . the money?"

Hob shook his head. "They found it at the back of the cave," he replied softly.

Brown took another gurgling breath and then his chest stilled. He died staring blankly at the night sky while Hob listened to the sounds of two horses descending the mountain.

CHAPTER 17

THEY gathered around the spring at dawn to prepare for the ride northward. Hob inspected the saddling of the horses. The buttermilk roan packhorse and the pair of horses belonging to John Frank Brown gave them just enough horseflesh to carry every member of their party.

Hob held a burlap bag with the stolen bank money while the men dug graves for Carl Tumlinson and John Frank Brown. When Shorty Stewart announced how he and the others planned to spend the money, Hob said, coldly, "It's going back to the bank in Abilene." A dangerous gleam in his eye warned the others to remain silent. "There've been enough men killed over this robbery loot, and I aim to see that it gets back to its rightful owner."

Not one of the men offered a word of protest. Young Scoop stared at his boots, unable to look Hob in the eye.

Don Miguel and Elena stood beside Hob until the shallow graves were finished. At Hob's insistence, they had placed John Frank Brown's body alongside the outlaw named Jack and covered it with a layer of stones. Carl Tumlinson's body was buried on the far side of the spring pool, because Hob felt the Texas Ranger would have wanted it that way.

"So it is with stolen property," Don Miguel said as he watched the graves being covered. "Someone must pay for it. These men have paid with their lives."

Hob hoisted the sack of money to his shoulder. "This money is going back to Abilene," he said. "If there's a reward, it'll go to Carl Tumlinson's family. My men will take no part of it. There's been enough trouble over it already."

Elena put her hand in the crook of Hob's arm. If Don

Miguel took notice, he gave no sign. "Your friends are alive," Elena said. "This is what matters most."

Hob shook his head, staring off at the canyon walls. "We've still got to find Mingus."

Elena searched Hob's face. "We will find him," she said with quiet assurance. "My father knows these mountains."

Hob tested his weight on the injured leg. Elena had cleaned the wound and bandaged it. The few inches of torn flesh would heal quickly. "It's the horses that worry me most," he said, with an eye on the gaunt flanks of the animals. "I hope they can carry us. It's a long stretch from here to the river, and I'm not leaving Mexico without my partner."

Don Miguel frowned, looking northward as the sky brightened above the canyon rim. "We will carry as much water as we can," he said thoughtfully. "At Agua Frio, there are wild javelina pigs near the spring. We can kill enough game so we will have food for ourselves, but it is the horses we must think of. It will be hard to find grass for our animals."

Hob thought about the ride back through the Chisos. "It'll be easier on the horses if we travel at night, when it's cooler. Let's head back to Agua Frio and see if we can rustle up a few wild pigs. The boys are ready. Let's get mounted."

The men assembled in front of Hob when the burying was finished. Shorty and Soap had little to say as Hob gave the signal to mount.

Before Hob stepped aboard the gray, he caught Elena by the arm. "Thanks again for what you did last night. I figure you saved my life when you winged the bounty hunter. I owe you."

Elena smiled. "Then you take back the remark about a woman carrying a gun?"

Hob nodded sheepishly, grinning. "Wish I hadn't said it," he mumbled.

She gave him a satisfied smirk, then turned for her horse, leaving Hob to face stares from the other cowboys. Hob glanced around at the group, then stepped quietly in a stirrup and pulled painfully into his saddle.

"Keep a sharp eye out for Mingus," he said, taking a last look at the silent canyon where the mystery of the hanged man had come to an end. Two fresh graves lay in the canyon now, the result of a letter found in a dead man's boot. "Hand me that letter," Hob said, directing his remark to Shorty.

"Ain't much use now," Shorty mumbled, fingering the sweat-stained envelope from his shirt pocket.

Hob took the letter and tore it to shreds. A soft breeze carried the pieces of paper away, scattering them across the canyon floor. "Let's ride," Hob said, reining toward the mouth of the canyon.

When they were through the narrow passageway, Elena heeled her mare alongside Hob. Hob glanced quickly to Don Miguel, expecting a look of disapproval when he saw them together.

Strangely, the old man smiled, then turned his face to the north and trotted to the front of the riders as they started along the wagon ruts toward Agua Frio.

Elena smiled and told Hob, "My father likes you. This morning he said you are a brave man, to risk your life for your friends. If you decide to visit our rancho in the fall, you will be welcome in my father's house."

In spite of his weariness after a night without sleep, Hob felt a tingle of excitement. "I aimed to come down to see you anyway," he said, "but I'm glad to hear your father won't have any objections to it."

Eyeing the dry, empty land around them, he was again filled with dread over his partner's fate. The Mexican desert was unforgiving. If Mingus had been unable to find water, he was doubtless afoot by now and possibly already dead from thirst.

Scoop rode up beside Hob and hung his head. "Sorry 'bout all the trouble we caused, Hob," he said. "We shouldn't have kept going like we did. I know'd it was wrong. I reckon we're in a peck of trouble with the boss."

Hob clamped his jaw to control his first impulse to snap angrily at the boy. "You're in trouble enough with me, on account of Mingus bein' out there lost. We can talk about it later. Right now, keep your eyes peeled for Mingus and help me find him."

Scoop sunk a little lower in the seat of his saddle and mumbled, "Yessir" as he reined away from Hob to ride with the others. Hob did not intend to be so hard on the boy, but he was boiling mad over the trouble the three Bar B men had brought to the ranch. Later, Hob's anger cooled some as he swept the barren peaks and valleys for sign of a rider. More than anything else Hob wanted to sight a lone horseman on a distant ridge, with the familiar slump-shouldered way of sitting a saddle.

They made a brief camp at nightfall to rest their horses and pass the canteens. It was a silent gathering, for the men understood Mingus's peril and Elena understood Hob's concern. In a few minutes, they were back in their saddles to make a night ride to the Agua Frio spring. Don Miguel rode out in front of their procession to scout the way. Through the night hours they made slow but steady progress across the mountains, following the wandering wagon road beneath twinkling stars.

Dawn found them an hour south of the spring. Hob spurred to the front of the procession to join Don Miguel.

"See anything?" Hob asked needlessly.

The old man shook his head, staring at the slopes in their path. "Perhaps farther north, my friend," he said, guiding his horse around a bend in the trail.

They approached the Agua Frio canyon a couple of hours past sunup. Hob found himself hoping with all his heart that they would encounter fresh tracks into the canyon mouth. As they rode toward the entrance Hob swept the ground with a careful look, but so many shod hoofprints had come in and out of the canyon, he could not make out a single set that might belong to Mingus. Hob took the lead as they trotted into the narrow passageway. Holding his breath, he hurried the tired horse around the bend into the box canyon.

At once he saw a horse tied in the shade beneath the trees beside the spring. Reflexively, his hand went to his gun butt as he slowed the gray for a more cautious approach. Then he heard a splash and saw someone floundering in the shallow pool. A slow grin spread over Hob's face, and his hand relaxed on the gun.

"I do believe that's the ugliest naked man I ever saw in my life!" Hob exclaimed, then burst out laughing as Mingus made a desperate run for his clothes on a rock beside the spring pool.

Hob dropped his reins to hold his belly, laughing uncontrollably. The laughter was pure relief, although Mingus did make for an unusual sight. His face and hands were browned by the sun, but the rest of him was the color of milk.

Mingus struggled quickly into his pants as Hob stepped off the gray and started toward him. Mingus gave Hob a lopsided grin when he drew near, listening to the other cowboys hoot and catcall from the far side of the canyon.

Standing in ankle-deep water and grinning as he buttoned his denims, Mingus shouted, "Mighty glad to see you, Hob."

The scar on Mingus's shoulder bore the marks of healing. Hob could never remember being so glad to see anyone before. He walked up to Mingus and stuck out his hand. "Glad to see you, too, partner," he said.

They shook hands, grinning at each other until the others rode up to the spring. Mingus quickly noticed Elena's presence and reached for his shirt, covering his bare chest self-consciously.

"You've got a bandage on your leg," Mingus said when he saw the strip of cloth around Hob's thigh. "How'd it happen?"

Hob hardly knew where to begin. "It's a long story. I can tell you everything on the ride back to the ranch. First off, tell me how you found this spring?"

"Followed that old road," Mingus replied quickly, pointing to the ruts across the canyon floor. "I see you found the boys all right. Did you get your hands on that money?"

Hob shook his head. "I've got it. Better'n five thousand dollars. We left two dead men back there . . . dead because of that robbery loot."

"Who were they?" Mingus asked softly, watching Hob's face. "Was one of 'em that Ranger?"

"Tumlinson got killed. We had him figured wrong. He was after the money to haul it back to the bank in Abilene."

Mingus's face clouded. "But he was the feller who bushwhacked us in those mountains?"

"No, the gent who shot you was a bounty hunter by the name of John Frank Brown."

Mingus nodded thoughtfully, then his face changed. "Sorry I went off like I did, Hob. Couldn't just lay there in bed whilst you and the men were off gathering cattle. I knew I could ride, and I figured our three friends were in some kind of trouble, so I saddled up and went after 'em. Looks like you found them before I could. Where'd the pretty lady and the old man come from?"

Hob tossed a glance over his shoulder at Elena. "Tell you on the way back," he said. "Meantime, best you get yourself dressed. This ain't Saturday, so how come you decided to take a bath today?"

Mingus grinned broadly. "Never was so glad to see water in my whole life, Hob. I might' near died out here yesterday, and that poor ol' sorrel hoss is just about done in. When I saw I couldn't drink this pool plumb dry, I decided I'd just lay down in it for a spell to see if I could soak some more of it through my skin."

Hob threw back his head and laughed. Soon the laughter

was infectious, spreading to the other men. Even Don Miguel burst out laughing.

Then Hob looked at Elena. Her smile made him forget the joy he felt at having found Mingus. Elena's beauty made him think of other things, until Don Miguel urged his horse closer to the spring.

"I will go hunting for wild pigs," the old man said. "If you build a fire, we can cook a meal and let the horses rest until it grows dark."

He pulled his rifle from its boot and turned his horse toward the passageway. Hob watched Don Miguel ride out of the canyon, thinking how much he owed him for his help finding the lost men in the mountains. Without his assistance, things could easily have turned out very differently.

They ate roasted strips of meat in the shade below the tree limbs, resting while the horses grazed on the meager grass across the canyon floor. The heat of the day passed slowly while everyone recounted the events of the past weeks.

As the stories were being told around the campfire, Hob looked around the fire at his companions and friends. The string of events that had begun when they found Dave Cobb's body on the banks of the Rio Grande was nearing an end. Mingus, Scoop, Shorty, and Soap were none the worse for wear—maybe seasoned a little by the experience, but all in one piece. Tom Barclay would be angry over the lost days of ranch work, but he would get over it with the help of Clara when she saw young Scoop Singleton returning home. All in all, things had worked out better than they might have, considering all the gunfire and the brutality of the desert. Hob was satisfied.

And there was Elena to brighten the prospects for his future. He remembered their whispered words that night as they sat side by side on his blankets, and the tender pressure of her lips when they touched his own. And he thought of what might develop between them when he visited the Montoya ranch this fall.

"Time we got saddled and headed north," he said. "We've got a long ride ahead of us and we'll have to take it slow, on account of the shape our horses are in. Let's get mounted, boys. There's work to be done on the Bar B, and a man waitin' for us who expects us to get it done as quick as we can."

If you have enjoyed this book and would like to receive details on other Walker Western titles, please write to:

Western Editor
Walker and Company
720 Fifth Avenue
New York, NY 10019